Secret Murder
Who Shall Judge?

"There is one problem. And here he comes, at this very moment."

Yes, Thorolf Pike was trouble. Declared an outlaw and exiled from his home, he had come from Surtsheim, where his fellow Norsemen lived, to Northlanding, where English settlers lived. Now he was dead, by an unknown hand. Who killed him? And, should the murderer be judged by English law, or by Norse law for the crime of secret murder?

SECRET MURDER

Who Shall Judge?

ELLEN KUHFELD

MONICA FERRIS PRESENTS
MINNEAPOLIS, MINNESOTA

With thanks to
Rebekah Sheely, who got me started
Mary Monica Pulver, who kept me going
Susan Henry, JW "Dub" Greenhill, and Monica Ferris,
who commented on earlier drafts
and the Aaardvark Writers' Group,
who lived through this with me.

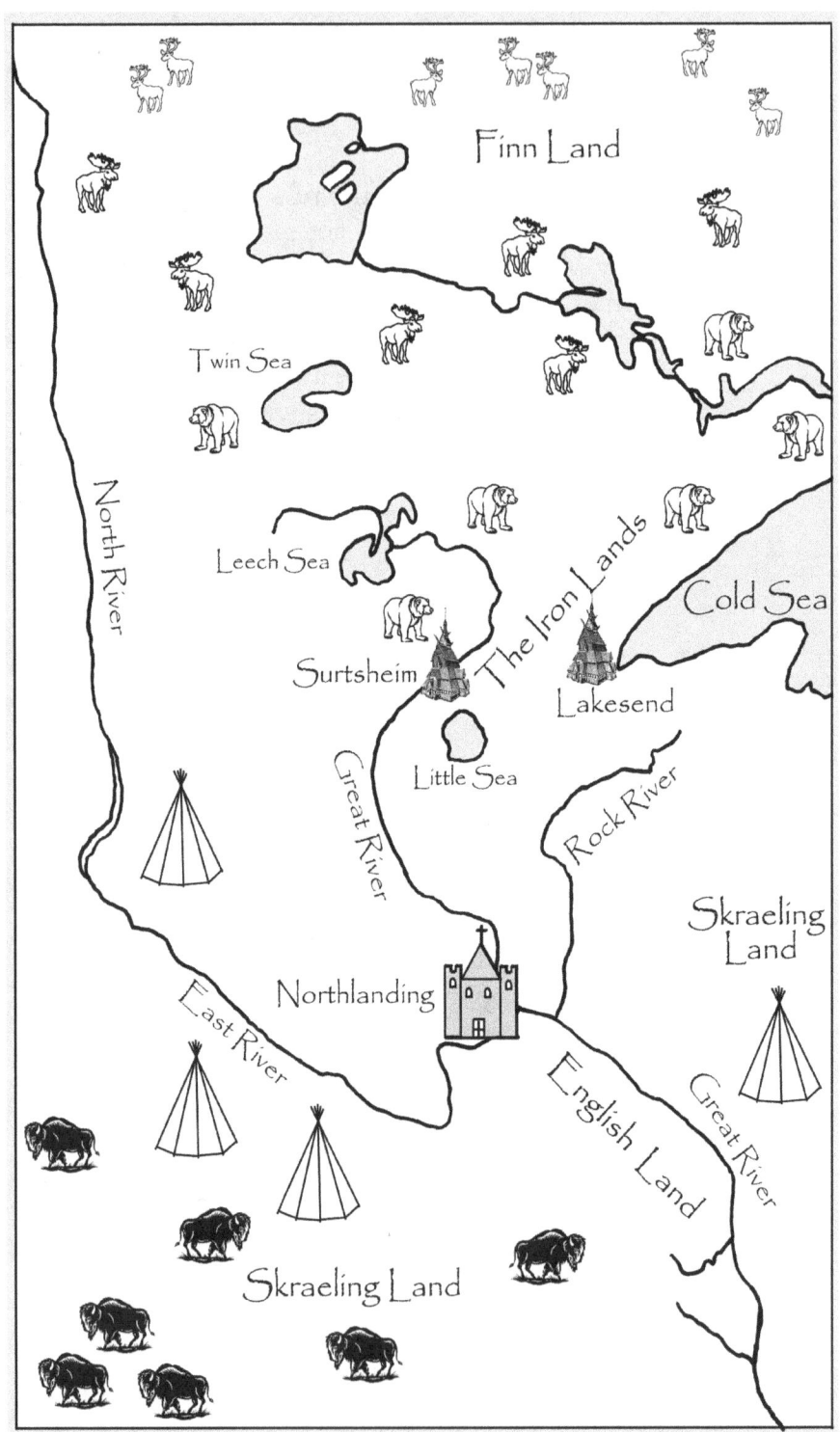

Prologue

Every Columbus Day, people argue about which European reached the Americas first. "Columbus didn't discover America, Leif Eriksson did!" The reply is usually, "It didn't work out for Leif, did it?"

History, archaeology, and the sagas tell a different story. Leif Eriksson didn't discover America, Bjarni Herjolffson did. The news spread, and about the year 1000, Leif Eriksson bought Bjarni's ship and went to explore this new land. He was delighted: Vinland was a *paradise*. (Leif came from cold Greenland, so his criteria for 'paradise' were easily met.) He went back to Greenland and told everybody about Vinland. His brothers joined in the exploration, and eventually the extended family tried to start a colony. The archaological traces at *L'anse aux Meadows* in Newfoundland may be the remnants of that colony. The Kensington Runestone is a questionable indication that the Norse even made it as far as Minnesota.

They didn't get along with the local people, whom the Norse called Skraelings. After a while, the Norse went away. They still visited Vinland to cut trees—timber was scarce and valuable in Greenland and Iceland—but they no longer tried to settle there. When the Little Ice Age came along, the North Atlantic got downright harsh. Europe lost contact with Greenland and Vinland. Columbus, taking a southern route far from the ice of the northern seas, rediscovered the New World.

But what if the settlements in the lands Bjarni discovered had taken root, and grown? What if more settlers, from the other lands of Europe, had poured in? There are more reasons for settlement than timber and furs. The Pilgrims came for religious freedom; others came to spread their faith. The Spanish came for gold. Some came because, for them, it was get-out-of-town or die.

The Americas would have developed very differently. There's always conflict when settlers move in on somebody's territory—but settlers from an eleventh-century Europe would have been on a relatively even footing with the Skraelings. They had iron, while the natives had flint and copper; but there were no guns to tilt the scales far off balance. The devastating plagues Columbus brought wouldn't be an issue—Europe wasn't plague-stricken until centuries after the Greenlanders' discoveries.

In the days of the Vikings, Muslims were invading and conquering southern Europe. They had Spain, they had southern Italy. In 846, they sacked Rome. They took the Caucusus, and they kept on expanding. In our world, they split into many countries, empires, and caliphates, then fell to fighting among themselves for supreme power. The Europeans were able to stop their territorial incursions.

But—what if Islam had kept on expanding, instead of quarreling? By the time Leif Eriksson came along, Christian Europe would have been eager for a quiet, peaceful New World to settle. From there, we can assume migrations proceeded somewhat as they did in our world, ending up with Spaniards and Portuguese in South America and Mexico, French at the lower end of the Mississippi, English and Dutch along the eastern seaboard of North America. English settlement could go west along waterways like the Ohio River, ending up at the Mississippi River.

Norse might settle the center of the continent—the first land they explored in the new world was Helluland, the 'land of flat rocks', commonly thought to be Baffin Island. If some had explored the Hudson Straits, home of seal, walrus, whale, and bear, the Norse would have discovered Hudson Bay. From there, they could travel by river to Lake Winnipeg, and further south along the Red River of the North and the other rivers of that region—routes the Voyageurs used in the fur trade. The Swedes, in particular, were great river travelers. The controversial Kensington Runestone suggests they took the Hudson Bay route as far as Minnesota.

We could end up with an Anglo-French empire along the Mississippi up to the head of navigation at Saint Anthony Falls. North of that would be Norse, settling on the Iron Range; and north of the Norse, Finns. Large areas of North America would still belong to the Skraelings. Traders would travel about, by land and by river, as traders always have. At trade fairs, men and women of different lands, laws, and customs would come together. As always, jackals would gather to prey upon them....

Chapter 1
Sunday: A Meeting with Trouble

"There have been rumors of thieves, yes indeed," Benedict said. "More rumors than usual."

Ragnar Forkbeard looked the trade booths over. They were about five paces wide, ten long, and there was fresh stonework and mortar at the top of the walls. *Clean and weather-tight,* Ragnar Forkbeard thought. Olaf Far-traveler, Ragnar's partner in this merchant venture, agreed. He smiled at the little agent. "Excellent job, Benedict! I see you've even had the walls heightened!"

"Strong men are your best protection, but strong walls are good also."

Ragnar looked back to the river, where his men were busy making sure the riverboats were well-grounded and moored. Nobody wanted them to get loose and go over the waterfall. "I think," he smiled, "I will go back to the boats and set our strong men to work carrying our goods inside of these strong walls. I'd hate to have thieves making free with my cargo."

Olaf grinned. "Haw! I'd like to see them running away with their booty!" Much of Ragnar's cargo was heavy bars of iron from the smelters of Surtsheim, though he had quite a few lighter items as well. Olaf had cloth and furs. His cargo was at greater risk.

Ragnar pointed. "I'll take the booth on the end nearer the river. You take the one on the other end, and we'll use the center booth for extra sleeping space and storage. Knute, you check everything out and make sure it's ready for us."

"Yes, Father."

Soon lines of men were carrying furs and fabrics into Olaf's booth and chests of knives, axes, arrowheads, and iron into Ragnar's. "Put the goods in the back," Ragnar said. "Set my bed up just this side of the wares." The man holding the carved dragon-posts leaned them against the wall and began fitting the sides of the bed to them and weaving the support cords together.

Other men tossed canvas over the roof-beams and snugged it down tightly. Gunnar, the cook, went directly to the cooking area. He had started a fire, and was making quick bannock bread to feed them all.

Ragnar saw a friend across the way: a burly man with dark hair and beard cut short, well-dressed in a tunic of yellow linen trimmed with interlacing embroidery at neck, sleeves and hem. They headed towards each other, and grasped shoulders warmly. "James! It's good to see you again!"

Ragnar paused, and examined the tunic. "But even dressed for trade you're at the anvil." His hand reached out to brush a small burn-mark.

"I went through the smithy on the way here," James explained. "One of the 'prentices was drawing out a bar with his fuller at an angle. I had to show him how to do it properly. Let a 'prentice learn the wrong motions, and it can take weeks to get them out of him. A spark must have flown in my direction."

"Don't those sparks always fly! Tell me, James, how have things been with you? Cecily was with child last time I was here."

James smiled. "A boy, strong and healthy, with his mother's eyes. We named him Mark. You can ask the same question next time, because Cecily is working on another. I just wish the business were as strong. I'm turning out more ironwork than ever. I have a new type of sword which is selling nicely."

"A new type of sword?" Ragnar interrupted.

"You've heard how the Saracens sometimes temper swords by heating them, then thrusting them into the belly of a slave? They say the swords take on the slave's life-strength. I don't know about that, but by all accounts such swords are uncommonly hard and tough.

"So I thought: if a sword can be improved by taking on the life of a slave, how about that of a bull? Bulls die for the butchers near my smithy in any case, but now they temper my blades in the process. The swords go for a premium, and I'm told by those who have used them that they hold their edge for an entire battle."

"It sounds to me as if your business should be doing very well," Ragnar said.

"There is one problem," James replied. "And here he comes, at this very moment." A cluster of men was approaching, led by a tall, wiry Northman with lank flax-colored hair. He was wearing a blue tunic embroidered with red and gold animals, and carried a polearm. All his men had swords, and two carried axes hooked over their shoulders as well.

Ragnar's face was neutral as the fourteen men stopped before him. "Thorolf Pike," he said to the Northman in the blue tunic.

"Ragnar Forkbeard," Thorolf Pike replied. The two looked at one another in silence. They were much alike in body, each half a head above the others. Thorolf had shaven chin and drooping moustache, thin mouth and cold blue eyes. Ragnar's hair was red-brown and thinning on top. His moustache flowed into his beard, which was neatly plaited in forks. He had seaman's wrinkles around his brown eyes, and still wore travelling clothes.

James Smith had quietly left, and Ragnar felt very much alone.

The man next to Thorolf spoke. He had red hair, and a face like a fox. "Nothing to say, then, Ragnar? Have you been studying the wisdom of Odin from the *Book of the High One?*

> The ignorant man had best stay silent
> When he moves among other men.
> None will know what a fool he is
> Until he begins to talk."

Ragnar flushed. "Let me finish that for you, Otkel.

> No man knows less what a fool he is
> Than the one who talks too much."

Thorolf Pike moved between the two. "Otkel! Be more polite to our friend." He turned toward Ragnar. "After all, he *is* a Northman in the lands of the English. He should be gladdened by the sight of men from his homeland."

Out of the corner of his eye, Ragnar saw James with Olaf Far-traveler. Olaf turned and signaled within his booth, and

Ragnar breathed more freely. "Thorolf, I am sure you have a reason for speaking with me, other than the joy of seeing a Northern face here in your exile."

"Why, yes," said Thorolf. "It seems to me that at recent fairs you've not been doing as profitably as you might. Perhaps you don't know these English traders well enough to protect yourself against their wiles."

"Who knows what can happen to a trader, alone among foreigners?" Otkel added with a sly grin. He was one of the men with an axe.

"And so, I am offering to conduct your trades for you," Thorolf continued. "I have lived among the English, and understand them. For a share in the profits, I am sure I can get you better prices. It is the least one Northman can do for another."

"I admit, I *would* feel at a disadvantage among the English, without Northmen to come to my aid," Ragnar agreed. "That's why I brought thirty Northmen with me." He gestured, indicating the area beyond the men facing him.

Thorolf and his men turned. Olaf and the crews of the boats had taken up weapons, come up silently, and stood in a semicircle behind them. Olaf smiled at Thorolf, then made the sign of Thor's Hammer—his fist across his chest, then down—as he was known to do before a battle. Gunnar, the cook, scowled at Otkel. Knute moved forward to stand by Ragnar.

"I like to think I'm a good trader, Thorolf," Ragnar's voice cut into the silence. "Humor me. If I'm right, I'll take the profit. If wrong, at least you won't take the loss. And now, I must oversee the storing of my wares."

Ragnar turned, and went to his booth. Thorolf and his men strode briskly off, though Otkel glanced several times over his shoulder. Olaf and the crewmen relaxed, and the normal bustle of setting up camp resumed.

"This sort of thing," Ragnar told his son, Knute, "is just *one* of the reasons you want your men to like you."

James was at their booths, and Ragnar thanked him for his help. "That could have gone badly if you hadn't called out my men, and Olaf's. It's bad enough that there are rumors of thieves, without adding Thorolf. How much trouble *has* he been causing?"

"Things were bad when his band arrived here six years ago, after Surtsheim outlawed them. They were pressuring all kinds of tradesmen, insisting on a share of their profits. Several merchants were beaten, and their families were threatened. Thorolf and his men promised to protect them from that kind of thing for a 'moderate' fee." James spat on the ground. "After that year Thorolf had enough money and influence to use silver, rather than violence, to lean on people. But nobody forgot. Thorolf and Otkel were good with the kind of smile that reminds you. These days, the way Otkel has been behaving, all the merchants are worried the threats and violence might start up again. And now I have a wife and a newborn son to protect."

"It'd worry me, too," Ragnar said sympathetically. "Thorolf may have been polite, but there was plenty of threat in the air just now, when I faced him and his men. And it wasn't all coming from Otkel, either. Hasn't the baron done anything about it?"

"All he seems to see is the wealth Thorolf gathers in. Thorolf's probably safe from the baron as long as he pays his taxes."

"I'm glad I live up north in Surtsheim district." Ragnar shook his head. "If it gets too dangerous down here, come to Surtsheim. I can always use another good hand in my smithy. Thorolf and his men *were* outlawed from Surtsheim after they killed Snorri Crow, so they won't come around threatening you."

"Your land and ways are too different. I don't think Cecily would be willing to go."

"Men can't do much about things like that. But at least we don't have a lazy baron up in the North."

By early afternoon, their goods had been put safely away. Half of Ragnar's bar iron was still in the riverboats, with samples stored among the chests of finished arrowheads, knives, and silver-inlaid axe-heads, the moose antlers and the silver jewelry. Olaf had his cargo of furs, and eastern fabrics from Miklagard. And the fair wouldn't fully start until tomorrow.

Ragnar was restless, anxious to be away from the fair-meadow, and thoughts of Thorolf, for a while. He changed into a green tunic with cream embroidery, and a rich yellow cloak which he fastened with a heavy silver brooch. He combed his hair and re-braided his beard, then put on silver arm-rings and bracelets. He transferred several small items from his chest to his pouch, donned his good sword-belt, and hung the pouch from it. He talked with his son Knute, told him to watch over the men and merchandise, then went to Olaf's booth.

"I sacrificed to Thor before we left Surtsheim," he told Olaf. "Now we are in Christian lands, and I should pay my respects to the White Christ."

"Off to visit your friends at the Abbey, then?"

"Yes. Abbess Margaret is a scholar—it's a pleasure to talk with her. And their steward, John Freemantle, knows a lot about the happenings in this town. He can speak from a viewpoint we'll not find among our fellow merchants here at the fair."

"Benedict says Thorolf stays away from churches except at Christmas and Easter, so he won't be there to bother you. Me, I'll stay here to make sure he doesn't steal the iron—boat and all." Olaf became serious. "Try to find out how Thorolf stands in the community these days, could you? We may have to do something about him."

"After this morning, be assured I won't forget Thorolf." And Ragnar went outside to claim a well-outfitted horse from Benedict's man.

Mounted, Ragnar stood high in the saddle and scanned the fairgrounds. Thorolf and his men were at the west end, talking to a trader in copper. Ragnar took the road to the south.

Carters and drovers filled the high-road to the fair. Porters carried bundles up the path to the left, slanting up the bluffs from the landing below the falls, then rested for a moment at the top. All the world was going to the fair, it seemed.

And all the world was going armed. This troubled him. The great falls was a border of sorts, and the Northmen from above came to trade with the English and the French from below. There was always tension when men of different lands gathered—but this fair was usually far more peaceful.

A great merchant rode by, with two dozen pack horses and half a dozen guards. A peasant with a sturdy knife thrust into his belt followed, driving hogs before him. *That knife looks like James's work,* Ragnar thought. There were a jester and a gleeman, armed only with their wits. Then came a well-dressed burgher with a sword swinging awkwardly at his side. Ragnar rode on, thoughtful.

He came to a small river. The road to Northlanding went ahead. Ragnar took the path to the right. He passed through a long forest hallway of trees and bushes, and was in another world.

There were sheep, herded into a milling mass to one side of the river, kept together by dogs and a circle of nuns all dashing back and forth. Men were in the stream, washing the sheep. Ragnar chuckled when one old ewe reared up, planted her hooves firmly in the shepherd's chest, and gave him a sudden dousing. Lambs bleated for their mothers, and shepherds watched over their cleanly flocks as they dried. In the distance, men were shearing and dressing with tar any wounds the sheep might have gotten in the process.

Not a one of them wore a sword.

Near the abbey was a small knot of men and women, the steward John Freemantle among them. He was dressed too finely for dealing with sheep—his clothes were a clear green, and had loose sleeves – but just right for dealing with servants. Ragnar rode to them, dismounted, and handed the reins of his horse to a villein. "Master John!" he said, smiling broadly.

John Freemantle broke free of his conversation, and strode over. He clasped Ragnar's hands. "Ragnar! It's good to see you! What manner of wares have you brought this year?"

"Iron, moose antler, knives, axes, and arrowheads. Silver jewelry. Olaf came too, bringing furs and cloth of Miklagard. The cloth should make fine vestments. And I see you will have much wool to trade."

"We must speak of this, later. But come! Lady Margaret is inside doing accounts on this fine day. She'll be glad of your interruption."

They were walking as they spoke, and as they passed the inner gate of the abbey John sent a servant to fetch the abbess. They sat on a bench in the shade of an oak, stretched, and talked companionably.

Abbess Margaret appeared with her crosier, accompanied by a novice carrying a silver ewer of warm water, a bowl, a carved wooden box of soap, and a fresh linen towel. The abbess was dressed no more finely than the novice, which said much about her.

"Abbess Margaret," Ragnar said.

"Master Ragnar," she replied, as she bent to wash his hands.

Ragnar quoted:

> Handcloths and a hearty welcome,
> Courteous greeting, then courteous silence
> That the traveler may tell his tale.

"You always have a saying, and it always seems to fit here," the abbess replied. "Are you sure your poets were not Benedictines in secret?"

"I choose my verses carefully, fitted to my surroundings. Peaceful lands bring forth peaceful sayings. I needed a stronger verse at the Fair. There is a great deal of tension there."

"It's Thorolf Pike," John Freemantle said. "He hasn't harmed anyone, hasn't even said anything that looks like a threat when written down. But he goes about with those men of his, and half the merchants in town are so frightened they let him broker their trading for them. The remaining merchants see the momentum Thorolf is getting, and the riches he's piling up, and are afraid of being trampled."

Ragnar flared his nostrils and made a sour face. "Thorolf has learned subtlety since he was outlawed from Surtsheim district. It must come from living in a land where they hang lawbreakers. But I can't say he sounds any better to live with."

"I wish you Northmen would hang your killers, instead of outlawing them. It would have saved us having to live with Thorolf."

"What, and then you'd want us to hang people that take the King's Deer? That's where it can end up, you know—though here on the borders, nobody much cares about deer yet."

A small brown monk had joined them: Father Hugh, the abbey priest. "I worry for the souls of our merchants. Surely many of them are considering desperate measures, which could easily lead to mortal sin."

Ragnar's eyebrows raised. "I should hardly consider measures taken against Thorolf to be a mortal sin."

Father Hugh frowned. "Such measures would be under-standable. But understandable or no, to answer his threats with violence would be a sin. I fear it will come to that."

Abbess Margaret made a gesture of distaste. "I see there are still advantages to living in cloisters. I had not heard of this man until now."

John and Ragnar laughed, and John said, "Such a blissful state should be preserved. Let us speak of other things!"

Ragnar opened his pouch. "It is good to once again see distant friends. Such moments should be celebrated with gifts." He drew forth a small meat-knife with staghorn handle. A silver cross was set into the horn, and silver runes decorated the blade. He gave it to John Freemantle.

Ragnar smiled. "I know rune-blades have a reputation for magic, and magic is not welcome among Christians. These runes say simply, 'Ragnar made me'. But if you wish to impress people, you need not tell them that."

For Abbess Margaret there was a string of prayer beads worked of polished hematite. "In the fires of the foundry," Ragnar said, "hematite becomes iron. Some say faith can be formed and strengthened in a similar manner. I thought you might appreciate the symbolism."

"And for you, Hugh, a cup." It was of soapstone, with a band of reindeer inlaid about the rim in alternating silver and niello. Father Hugh's plain face filled with delight, for he loved both animals and wine.

"I couldn't ask for a finer gift!" He filled the cup with burgundy from the south, raised it to his mouth, and drank. As he was setting it down, the conversation became interesting. He gestured, the cup lurched and spilled over, and there was a dark new burgundy stain on his habit to keep the old stains company.

The abbess raised her eyes to the heavens, and the novice hurried up with her hand-towel, soap, and water. Ragnar and John laughed. "It's yours, Hugh, it's truly your cup now," John said.

"Like Father, like son," Ragnar added. And so the afternoon passed, in conversation and laughter.

A bell spoke, and the abbess rose. "It's time for vespers. Will you join us for worship?"

Ragnar stood. "That's one of the reasons I came." And together they went into the small church: Father Hugh to the lectern, Abbess Margaret to the choir, Ragnar and John to the pews.

"*Deus, in adjutorium meum intende,*" Father Hugh intoned. "*Domine, ad adjuvandum me festina,*" the congregation replied. "*Gloria Patri, et Filio....*"

The rolling phrases went on. The church was comfortably warm, and the candles were just beginning to show against the bright twilight shining through the windows of colored glass. Ragnar did not understand Latin, had not been raised with it, but the holy pictures of the windows spoke to him.

"*...Tu es sacerdos in aeternum....*"

One window caught his eye: a powerful bearded man with a hammer, light shining about his head. Could it be Thor? Many of the people back in Surtsheim worshiped the White Christ—though belief in Him was not as strong as it had grown in the days before the Saracens took Rome and sent the Christians fleeing. Perhaps the Christians were learning to believe in Thor, as many Northmen had learned of Christ? Both gods were strong for protection and generosity. They made a good pair.

No, he decided. That was a carpenter's hammer, not a war hammer. It had to be the Christ, or perhaps his father Joseph. Both had been carpenters. Still, the images of Thor and Christ came together in his mind.

I must talk with Father Hugh of this, he thought, as Father Hugh turned and gestured, in movements solemn and formal as a pavane. *I'll consider speaking with Abbess Margaret after I hear what Hugh has to say.*

The service had drawn near its end as Ragnar mused. He joined the others in the final *amen,* then rose and left the church with John Freemantle.

The sun was almost down, and the long northern twilight of May filled the air. Clouds above shone brilliantly, from heights the shadows of evening had not yet reached.

"I must go now," Ragnar said. "The light lasts a long while, this time of year, but it's a considerable distance back to the fairgrounds." John whistled and waved, and a villein brought up Ragnar's horse. Ragnar mounted.

"Visit us at the fair," he told John, "and be sure to bring a wool sample so we can speak of trade with all the goods handy for inspection." He waved farewell, and the horse cantered out along the path.

Ragnar passed through the woods. As his horse was about to turn onto the fairgrounds road, he reined it back into the concealment of the bushes. *Well, well,* he thought. *What have we here?* And he took his bow from its case upon the saddle.

Only the darkest blue was coloring the heavens, and the stars were out, when Ragnar saw the campfires of the fair glowing against the treetops ahead. He led his horse to the fire where perhaps a dozen of his men were lounging. Instead of going directly to the paddock, he went into the darkness between two of the booths. He motioned Gunnar to follow him.

There was a form on top of the horse, covered by Ragnar's cloak. He lifted the cloth to reveal as plump a buck as ever one could wish for, at least in the spring. "He came to the edge of the woods at twilight, as deer will do, so I shot him. Don't you think venison stew would help sustain us through tomorrow's trading?"

Gunnar's teeth gleamed in the shadow of his beard. "Stew it'll be, and I'll make sure nobody sees me doing the butchering—especially the gamekeepers. They don't seem to care that much about the King's Deer in Northlanding, but there's no sense tempting Fate."

Ragnar went back to the fire, leaving the horse and the buck to Gunnar. He made a quick guess where the best balance would be between smoke and mosquitoes. Two men scooted apart to make room for him in the circle.

He rolled his cloak into a cushion and leaned against it. Knute handed him a horn of ale. He drank. "Ah!" he sighed, and was quiet for a while as he listened to one of the men telling the tale of Thor and the giant Thrym. He thought it well done, and joined in as the crew applauded afterwards.

I must tell a saga soon, Ragnar said to himself. *Perhaps the history of Duke William? But not tonight—there is no patience for saga, the first night at the fair. Less than half the men are here at our fire.*

A woman's laughter drifted across the camp. Smiling, Ragnar remembered the days before he had married, then rose and stretched his bones, which had stiffened from sitting on the ground. He picked his way past sleeping Northmen to get to his waiting bed.

He unbuckled his sword, hung it on the bedpost, took off his clothes, lay on one bearskin and pulled the other over him. Nights could be cold, this close to the river. From outside there was a burst of drunken Norse song—some of the men back from the tavern, no doubt. The interwoven ropes creaked beneath him as he rolled on his side. He slept.

Chapter 2
Monday: Thorolf's body, Thorolf's men

Mist shrouded the trail as Benedict rode from Northlanding toward the fairgrounds. Several pack-horses laden with food supplies and trade goods followed, led by two men still half-asleep. Benedict was quite awake: his night watchman always roused him as soon as light quickened in the east. He had dressed in working-merchant's clothes, eaten his breakfast of sops in wine, and spent a moment in prayer, by the time the rest of the household was stirring.

Don't they realize the first full day of the fair is no time for lying abed? he thought, as he looked back at his little caravan. *So much to do, and only a week to do it!*

Suddenly his horse shied, dancing sideways toward the river. The other horses seemed alarmed, too. Benedict and the men fought them back under control. "Hob! Joseph! Do you see anything to upset them? Pest and bother! Blast this fog!" But nothing seemed amiss, and the horses were avoiding a spot closer than the woods looming dimly at the edge of vision.

Probably not a bear, Benedict thought as he dismounted and they tied the horses—but he had his sword, Hob his staff, and Joseph his whip as they went to investigate.

Thorolf Pike lay in the tall grass between the trail and the woods. Droplets of morning dew spangled the gray-goose fletching of the arrow piercing his side. His neck was bent unnaturally, and his crumpled form looked as if he'd been thrown by a horse—thrown far.

Benedict was stunned for an instant, then took command. "We're almost to the abbey road. Take my horse, and tell Father Hugh a man is in need of the final sacraments," he snapped at a no-longer-sleepy Hob. "You, Joseph—run and fetch the bailiff! I'll stay here to watch the body!" He listened to the sound of hoofbeats and running feet fading into the mist.

"Heavens above!" he murmured as he returned to the packhorses, and neatened up their reins tied to a tree on the far side of the trail. "What next?" he said as he returned to stand perhaps ten feet from Thorolf's body. In the chill air, he wished he had warmer clothes. He pulled up his hood, and sought as much warmth as his shoulder-cape could provide.

Benedict wondered if it had been wise to call upon Father Hugh. Thorolf had not been a good Christian, and he looked extremely dead. The last rites were for those yet living. Still, there was argument about when the soul left the body. The sacraments of the Church could do no harm in any case. Father Hugh was the sort of priest who would bless a body from which the soul had fled, rather than risk failing to bless a body with the soul still in it. He would even bless a primsigned man like Thorolf, who'd only been told of the Christ and had the sign of the cross made at him, but showed no sign of real conversion.

In silence and fog, Benedict examined the scene. The grass around Thorolf seemed untouched. The road and roadside had gotten heavy use the previous day. It was hard for him to tell, but he thought the soft ground showed a horse had reared and bucked in panic, then run. Near these marks lay Thorolf's polearm. Thorolf's hair, eyelashes, flesh, and clothes were covered with dew. He looked as if he'd been completely undisturbed since he had fallen.

There was the sound of a running horse. Could the bailiff be coming already? A rider loomed out of the mist, then reined to a sudden stop: a merchant from the south, by his clothes. He looked at the body. "God's teeth, it *is* Thorolf Pike! The runner I met was right!"

Benedict stepped between the horseman and the corpse. "Just don't disturb things. I'm trying to keep the body as it is, until the bailiff can see it."

The merchant laughed. "Thorolf can't disturb *me* any longer, so I'll return the favor. But people at the fair will want to know of this!" He slapped his horse on the rump and they were off, quickly vanishing into dimness.

Hoofbeats again, two pairs of them from the direction of the abbey. Hob rode up, followed by Father Hugh on his little donkey. Hugh dismounted, fetched a box from his panniers, and trotted over to Thorolf's side. Quickly, he draped his stole about his neck and tucked it under his cincture, then began setting up a small table for the anointing. He knelt beside Thorolf, closed his eyes in prayer for a moment, and began. *"Adjutorium nostrum in nomine Domini...."*

The little priest, immersed in the sacraments, was alone with Thorolf. Benedict was watching this world as well as the next, and the day was beginning. The mist was burning off, and more people were coming up the trail from Northlanding toward the fair. They stopped, and formed a circle at a respectful distance from Hugh, who was anointing Thorolf's eyes, nose, mouth. They were silent, but as Hugh said the last "Amen," a buzz of conversation broke out.

"It's Thorolf!" "Somebody finally did something about him!" "Hi, there's his polearm, over in the weeds." "Where were all those men of his?" "I think I'll get off to the fair and see about doing some trading—without his help, for once." "Isn't that the bailiff coming?"

Six troopers thundered up, and began chasing the crowd off. It was a hopeless task—the day was fully begun, and people were arriving as rapidly as they could be dispersed. Dirk Cachepol, the bailiff's deputy, glanced at Father Hugh and held in his curses. He set one trooper to handle the horses, and the others in a line to keep traffic moving past, well away from the body. Rumpled, face covered with salt-and-pepper stubble, Dirk looked as if the messenger had caught him asleep. That didn't fool Benedict. It was hard to catch the deputy asleep, even harder to catch him with a shave.

The line parted, and a horseman on a sleek bay gelding rode through. The bailiff had arrived. Gervase Rotour was tall, with black hair, moustache, and a shaven chin. He had a small paunch. He wore huntsman's clothes of green and brown particolor, simple but of the finest fabric. His rings were of massive dull-finished gold. His aristocratic nose wrinkled slightly at the smell of Thorolf warming in the sun.

Dirk Cachepol came to his side, and the bailiff suddenly looked even more elegant and subtle by contrast. Dirk took the reins as the bailiff dismounted. Gervase came up to perhaps three paces from the body, and studied it. "Definitely murder. What have you learned so far?"

"When Benedict found the body—" Dirk motioned toward a small cluster of men and horses, a donkey and a priest "—Thorolf was lying there dead as Pontius Pilate. Dew had settled on his hair and clothes. Tracks say his horse was startled—threw him high, then ran back to the road. Thorolf dropped his polearm when that happened. And an arrow never bent his neck at that angle. I figure it broke when he landed. That's why he's so far from the road, he was thrown."

"Father Hugh is the only one actually touched the body, giving last rites. He left out anointing Thorolf's feet so he wouldn't muss up his shoes. He also testifies to the dew.

"Thorolf still has his silver arm-rings, and his sword. Now that you're here...." Dirk broke off and went over to the body. He knelt, untied Thorolf's pouch, then spilled its contents into his hand. Silver coins and hack-silver rolled out into an impressive pile.

"Robbery was not the reason for this killing," the bailiff agreed. "And nobody in his right mind would openly confront a horseman carrying a polearm. Thorolf was killed from ambush, by an enemy. Which way was his horse going?"

Dirk pointed toward Northlanding, away from the fair. "It looks like he was returning home."

Gervase took possession of the pouch and silver. "The arrow was in his right side. It probably was shot from those bushes, somewhere from *there* to *there*. Have the men search, and bring me everything that's not rooted in the soil."

The bailiff went over to the onlookers. "Murder has been done here, and I am determined to find the criminal. If a person were to step upon evidence, say—even accidentally—I would have to interview them to find the nature of that which they had damaged. We're busy, and that could take some time, so I must ask for your cooperation in keeping people well away from the body."

He turned, saw some of the troopers poking gingerly around the edges of the bushes. He raised his voice: "You're looking for signs of an ambush on open ground, hm? Get in there, and get to work!"

Gervase went back to Dirk as the onlookers gave the scene a wider berth. "Subtlety, Dirk, always subtlety. Nobody wants to be held as a witness, especially the week of the fair. That'll keep them away better than a line of troopers." They watched the men carefully picking their way among the underbrush for a moment, and then Gervase walked over to Thorolf's body.

He knelt and took the corpse's arm: stiff. But Thorolf's legs were still limp. He examined the arrow—certainly a heart shot—then pulled it out. It had penetrated deeply. The head was a type favored among the Northmen. The fletching was of gray-goose pinions. The identifying cresting had been scraped off completely, probably with the edge of a knife.

He stood, wrapped the bloody arrow in cloth, and looked about for a place to put it. It was a yard long, too long for his saddlebags or his scrip. He tucked it in his belt. Then he and Dirk watched the searchers return empty-handed. "Nothing, my lord, not even footprints. The ground is rocky, and if a man were careful he could move without leaving traces."

"Set guards to make sure nothing is disturbed. Somebody go back to Northlanding for a wagon to carry the body." With that, the bailiff drew Dirk Cachepol to one side, where they could speak privately.

"Not very much evidence here," Dirk grumbled.

"Oh, we've learned a fair bit," the bailiff replied. "Thorolf was killed by an enemy, from ambush, using an arrow with a Northman's arrowhead. There was dew on his clothing, and he's started to stiffen, so he's been here some while. If he were killed when there was light and traffic, his body would have been discovered earlier, but the arrow was well-aimed, so it couldn't have been dark. Somewhat after sundown, I'd say, but well before the moon or stars were out.

"He was probably coming from the fairgrounds. We'll have to look for his horse. And he usually travels with a number of men. I wonder where they were? Set somebody to finding out."

Gervase sighed. "Thorolf has been a nuisance, but a well-mannered one. This is unlike him. The last thing we need is for one of the richest local merchants to be found murdered on the first day of the trade fair.

"Wasn't Thorolf outlawed from Surtsheim district some years back? He must have many enemies there. And three boats from Surtsheim landed just yesterday. Three boatloads of Northmen for suspects, Dirk—thirty or so of them. That's excessive."

"Three boatloads of *rich cargo* and suspects, m'lud," Dirk added.

"Thank you, Dirk. You do have a grasp on such things. Hm, the baron *will* insist justice pay for itself—and we haven't collected many fines lately, have we?

"Let's go see if we can catch a killer."

Dirk stood tall a moment, then pointed down the road toward Northlanding. "At least we won't have to look for Thorolf's men," he said. "Here they come now, all fancied up like the boar's head at a feast."

Gervase shaded his eyes. "Your vision is sharper than mine. But that seems to be the ceremonial wagon from the Northmen's sacred grove, and they'd be the ones wanting it for Thorolf."

They watched the men and wagon approach. The crowd made way for them in silence, though there was a buzz of conversation farther away. Ten stopped their horses with the wagon, near Thorolf. Otkel and two others rode up to the bailiff and dismounted.

Otkel wore a blue tunic with silver embroidery, white breeches with blue cross-garters, boots, and a short cape of white bear-fur from the land of the Finns. His arms and fingers were covered with silver rings. Around his neck was an amulet of a one-eyed man. Gervase thought he had never seen Otkel looking so handsome, or so dignified.

It takes a funeral to bring out the best in some, the bailiff thought. "It is a sad occasion," he said aloud.

Otkel replied. "We've come for Thorolf, but first, tell us what has happened here. The stories we've heard can't all be true."

"Benedict found the body at sunrise. He immediately sent for me and for a priest, who gave Thorolf the final sacraments. As far as we can tell, Thorolf was killed between sundown and night, by an arrow shot from ambush. He was not robbed.

"You may be able to answer some of the remaining questions. Thorolf usually traveled about with you and the other men, yet no cry was raised last night. Either he was alone, or with an accomplice of the killer. How did he come to be separated from you?"

A look of pain crossed Otkel's face. "He sent us away. We were at the fair most of the day, negotiating sales. About an hour before sundown he told us to go back to Northlanding, to make sure the promised shipments were arriving at our warehouse and the servants were taking proper care of them. 'I have one piece of business that won't need your help,' he said."

"I thought you all shared in business. Why would he prefer you not be there for some of the negotiations?"

Otkel smiled with half his mouth. "I think this business was with a woman. Who among us is fond of women that are shared?"

"Hm," said the bailiff, then he was silent for a moment. "Men have killed before, over women. Do you think that's happened here?"

"How should I know?" For a flash, Otkel was his old self again: querulous, suspicious. "We don't even know it was a woman—we're only guessing."

Gervase spread his hands in a calming gesture. "You've pointed to a trail. We'll send the hunters out, and see what game they find.

"I wonder, also, what happened to Thorolf's mount. A frightened horse heads for his stall—and this one was frightened enough to throw Thorolf. You surely would have been out searching had the animal come home without the man. The killer may have made his escape on Thorolf's horse, which could be a very important clue."

Otkel's eyes widened. "You'd have to be brave and nimble to catch Storm when he was panicked, let alone ride him—few besides Thorolf could handle him at the best of times. But we haven't seen Storm since yesterday, so you may be right."

The bailiff smiled. He was learning a great deal from Otkel, and in the distance he could see his men talking quietly with Thorolf's men. They would come together to weave the larger picture, after the Northmen had gone. But for now, Otkel was his chief concern.

He took the arrow from his belt. When he unwrapped it, the blood had dried so it could be handled freely. He showed it to Otkel and the other two. "This is the arrow that killed Thorolf. Does anything about it seem familiar?"

Otkel took the arrow, turned it over in his hands, sighted along the shaft, checked the nock and fletching. He examined the head carefully. "Give me that cloth, will you?" he asked the bailiff absently, and used it to clean away the crusted blood.

"This arrowhead was made by Ragnar Forkbeard," he said. "See, there, that rune? That's his mark. Ragnar and his men have been sworn foes to us for six years and more. They were the main force behind our outlawry from Surtsheim. They've shed our blood before."

The bailiff thought of one of Ragnar's men, found dead year before last; and he'd heard of Snorri Crow's death. He didn't let it show on his well-schooled face. "You've told me many things," he said to Otkel. "I see no further reason to detain you in your grief. One of my men will come with you, to aid you in whatever ways he can. If you think of anything else I should hear, tell him."

He motioned over a grizzled old veteran named Rhys. "Go with Otkel. Help him however you can." *And watch these wild Northmen to make sure they don't take things into their own hands,* he thought to himself. He knew Rhys would understand without being told.

Otkel and the other Northmen went to Thorolf's body. The sun was high now, and the carvings on the wagon were a brilliant pattern of interlaced highlights and shadow. The trees and bushes were the vivid green of spring, and all of the Northmen were dressed very handsomely. They seemed more a tapestry picture than ordinary life.

Four of the men lifted the rounded body of the wagon off its undercarriage, and placed it beside Thorolf. It was lined with a cushion of furs and rich cloth. They laid him down on that cushion. There was some trouble over his legs, which were beginning to stiffen. They placed his head upon a pillow, and covered him with a blanket of deepest red.

Otkel straightened the body's head, combed its hair, neatened its mustache. "Come, Thorolf," he said quietly. "It's time for your last journey." He and three others lifted the wagon and its load, carried it over, and snugged it into place between the wheels. Each took a braided rope of red leather, and tied his corner of the wagon-bed to the carved heads at the ends of the frame. Then they set Thorolf's polearm, straight up, into a socket at the side.

A Northman mounted one of the wagon's team horses. The others were ready to ride escort. The crowd moved back to give them clear passage. Suddenly a look of surprise crossed Otkel's face, as if something unseen by others rose up before him. He signaled the Northmen to stop, then dismounted and returned to the wagon.

He bowed his head. His fist traced a pattern in the air before his chest: across, then down. "Pardon the intrusion, Thorolf, but this is important." He lifted the blanket, examined the corpse.

His face whitened, then flushed. "To be killed by an enemy is one thing—but to be killed by a thief...." His voice was low, but forceful; the other Northmen heard, but none of the crowd did. He neatly covered Thorolf again, tucked the blanket in, then turned and walked to the bailiff.

"Matters have changed," he said without preamble. "Thorolf may have been robbed after all—he had a pouch with a great deal of silver when he left us, and it's nowhere on his body. I would look for enemies from the north—but a thief may be from anywhere."

Gervase Rotour was silent for a moment, then spoke. "Your powers of observation do you great credit, Otkel. But he had his pouch. I have taken it as King's Evidence that he was not robbed, alongside the arrow that killed him."

Otkel's silence was longer than the bailiff's. Finally: "Your king is welcome to his evidence, for as long as he needs it. There will be enough silver for Thorolf's pyre in any case." He turned abruptly and walked back to his horse. The wagon began to roll, six Northmen preceding it and six behind. It looked for all the world like a noble travelling in state with a band of retainers. Rhys followed at a discreet distance.

Gervase shook his head, and spoke to Dirk. "We're going to have trouble from Otkel. We'd best find the killer while the Northmen are busy with Thorolf's funeral. Otherwise, who knows what they'll do?

"Gather our men. We can talk on the way to the fairgrounds."

Gervase went to Benedict's little group. "Many thanks for your help in this matter, and for staying in case you were needed. Now it's time for me to investigate elsewhere. You are free to go about your business."

Hob and Joseph began untying the pack horses, while Father Hugh tried to untangle his donkey's reins from the bushes they had somehow gotten woven in with. "Bless your mission, bailiff," he said over his shoulder. "There's a murderer among us, and suspicion eats at the soul. Catch him. Set our minds at peace."

The reins came loose. The donkey, sensing he was free, brayed and dashed away. Father Hugh went after him, habit flapping against his legs, crashing through the bushes. He caught a rein, then went tumbling on the ground in the process. He rose, dusted himself off, prayed vigorously to Saint Jerome for patience, and began admonishing the animal. The crowd, its tension released, laughed immoderately.

Benedict pulled his group together, Hugh spoke firmly, and the bailiff and his men rode off toward the fairgrounds. The crowd began to mill about. Some clustered where Thorolf's corpse had lain. Others left.

All day long people stopped, drawn by the gawpers already there, were told what had happened, and in the process themselves drew more curious travelers. They, in turn, explained to the newcomers. The site was not deserted until the stars began to show, and some of the tales told by evening were truly strange and wonderful.

Chapter 3
Monday: Matilda and the Tavern

Gervase and his men rode slowly, talking. Horseback can be a very private place, and they had much to say among themselves.

The bailiff spoke first. "We have to find Thorolf's horse, and Otkel said he thought Thorolf stayed at the fair to meet a woman. Finding her is, like as not, our most important job."

"That won't be hard," one of the troopers said. "It's Matilda, the widow who runs the stables in Milltown. She has horses to rent at the fairgrounds."

Gervase raised his brows. "Otkel didn't know that."

"Otkel may be a fine lieutenant—but would you tell him the secrets of your soul? Leif knew of Matilda. He's the stocky Northman with the red beard and crucifix. The others seemed shaken from loss of leadership in a foreign land. Leif, I think, mourned a friend."

"It must have been lonesome, being Thorolf," the bailiff mused.

"Leif seemed to think that, too. But Matilda was always pleasant to Thorolf. She's from Milltown, so he didn't see her nearly as often as he spoke of her. They met again yesterday, and Leif says Thorolf was absent-minded afterwards. He sent the rest of them back to Northlanding like a man who's made up his mind."

"We'll leave our horses at Matilda's paddock," Gervase said decisively. "I want to see her.

"Now, we must plan the rest of our investigations. Matilda might solve this for us—but when have we ever been fortunate enough to have the answer drop into our laps like that, hm?"

"Last fall. Remember we stopped at the Dancing Bear to ask if travelers had seen the robber we were after? And there he was, drunk as a monk in the corner." Dirk had a weakness for interrupting.

"Hm. Thank you, Dirk. That's once, men, once in the last year. The rest, we had to work for." The bailiff paused a moment. "And Dirk has told me how we will go about it.

"We can speak directly with Matilda—but Ragnar is a formidable man, and has a large crew. We'll want more information before we discuss Otkel's accusation with him. Ragnar knows Dirk and myself, so the rest of you will have to investigate him.

"Dirk and I will be at the tavern. You'll know where to find us, and taverns are filled with active tongues. We should pass the time profitably."

Planks echoed as their horses crossed a small wooden bridge and came onto the fairgrounds proper. They turned to the left, and rode toward Matilda's paddock.

The fair covered the meadow like Joseph's coat come to life. Merchants, porters, locals, beggarmen dressed in clothes of many hues, lands, conditions, and estates mingled in harmonious disputation. A juggler held a small crowd spellbound, and children clustered about an old storyteller. A sweetmonger with pots of honey and cakes of maple sugar was bargaining vigorously with the Master of the local bakers' guild as they passed his booth. The clangor of an anvil resounded.

Somewhere, Gervase knew, thieves were waiting for opportunity. And perhaps one person in all this multitude was a murderer.

Patches of brightness and color before them clarified into bolts of cloth, spread out on a pattern of ropes surrounding a tent. A merchant, his clothes an advertisement for his wares, stood among them gesticulating with a stooped little tailor. Beside him was a woman selling needles and bright threads for embroidery to a woman who looked to be local.

They rounded the clothseller's display, and the paddock was before them. A split-rail fence enclosed an area of beaten grass, holding perhaps a dozen horses and capable of holding thrice that. A thatched roof covered several box stalls and a small shed at the rear. In the shade of the roof, a woman sat on an overturned bucket, leaning sideways against a stall.

When she saw them approaching, she rose and came gracefully forward. She was slim above the waist, with broad hips. Her blue overdress was girdled up, showing a white underdress. Auburn hair cascaded beneath her white kerchief. Her face was pleasant, but her eyes were very tired.

"How may I be of service, good gentles?" she said in a soft voice.

"Our horses must be taken care of," Gervase answered. "Fed and watered, but left saddled in case we need them suddenly." He dismounted, as did his men.

She took the reins of Gervase's horse, touched her hand to its cheek, spoke quietly in its ear. She opened the gate, and the big bay walked docilely into the paddock.

The bailiff smiled in approval. *This woman is good with horses!* She led the bay to a trough of water, and a manger filled with hay. The other horses, clearly jealous, crowded into the strange enclosure with very little prodding.

Dirk grasped the bailiff's sleeve, and whispered in his ear. "That's Thorolf's horse, Storm, in the center stall." The aroma of garlic sausage filled Gervase's nostrils.

Matilda returned, closing the gate behind her. "Care of seven horses would be threepence ha'penny the day," she said, "and since you may be leaving suddenly, I'll have to ask for payment in advance."

Gervase opened his pouch for the coins, and gave them to Matilda. *For such a small hand, how strong it is,* he thought. "I'm looking for a special horse, and I believe you may have just the one." He gestured toward the center stall, and Storm.

"That horse is lame," Matilda said. Her eyes, which had been tired, glistened. Gervase realized she had begun to cry.

The bailiff took her gently by the shoulder and led her to a pile of hay, sat her down, made her comfortable. She turned her head to lean on the fencerail; and though Gervase could not see her face, he could tell by her breathing that she still wept silently.

He gestured to his men. One went to examine Storm, while others dispersed into the crowd that was beginning to form. Word of Thorolf's death was everywhere—and here was the bailiff with a weeping woman. Tongues were sure to wag: troopers in the crowd could hear a lot, and help control things, if need be.

At last Matilda gulped, and her breathing became regular. She straightened up, and wiped her eyes with the tails of her kerchief. She was alone with the bailiff, with a circle of watchers at perhaps a rod's distance.

"I'm sorry, my lord. I've known since last evening that I was in terrible trouble. Today I learned the trouble was different than I thought. When you spoke to me, you caught me off-balance."

Gervase smiled sympathetically, and kept his silence. He was an exceptionally talented listener, Matilda was talking, and there would be time for questions later.

"My husband, Gib, died of a fever six years ago. That was about the time Thorolf and his men came to Northlanding. I kept up the stables and paddock – I already was doing most of the horse-training, it's something women are good at.

"Thorolf sometimes rented horses from me, in the early days before he'd settled on his course of business. We got along well, but we were both too filled with our sorrows—me a widow, he an exile—for it to go beyond that.

"And then he began insisting that merchants take him as a trading partner. A number of people were badly beaten. He's been able to get along with quiet threats ever since."

She was silent a moment. "I guess that's all over now, isn't it?

"I didn't approve, but he would visit the stables now and then, and I would be pleasant. He wanted to trade in goods that could be kept in his warehouses—not horses—so he was no danger to me as long as I didn't anger him. Politeness works with horses, and it seemed to work with Thorolf. I did not realize he'd taken it for something more.

"Yestereve I was in the shed working on tack when Thorolf came to see me. We spoke for a while, then he embraced me and said I would be his."

Matilda's eyes were unseeing, looking at a different place and time. Gervase thought she might be of two minds in this matter: lonely, wanting Thorolf despite knowing what he was. She continued.

"I told him he could not have me—and he tried to force me. I work with horses, I am stronger than I appear. We had a set-to, which panicked Thorolf's horse. He sprained himself.

"That brought Thorolf and myself to our senses. I loaned him one of my horses, so he could return home, and promised to care for Storm until he was healed. He rode off, and that is the last I saw of him. The last thing he said to me was that we would speak further of this on the morrow.

"I realized Thorolf now thought I had betrayed him. God alone knows what he would have done! I put Storm in a box stall, then went to the tavern. And that's all I remember, until I awoke this morning."

"What about the horse you lent Thorolf?" Gervase asked.

"He was in the paddock this morning—but I don't remember anything about it. When I saw him there, I assumed Thorolf had turned him loose to make his own way home. Thorolf kept other horses at his warehouse, so he wouldn't have needed mine."

"A plain story, Matilda, forthrightly told. But you say you have no memory of the time of the murder. This is a matter for concern, hm?"

Matilda snorted. "I may not have the memory, but I have the hangover. Ask at the tavern, I'm sure they can speak for me there." She rose, addressed the watching crowd. "Good neighbors, I am sure many of you saw what happened yesterday. An' you love me, tell the bailiff truly what happened."

She sat again on the hay, leaned against the fence. "I place my fate in their hands, bailiff. I can say no more."

Gervase Rotour motioned to one of his men. "Stay with her. Watch her, protect her." He went forth into the crowd.

An old gaffer, with keen ears for his age, nudged the bailiff. "Heh, 'set-to.' Bailiff, it did these old eyes good. All the brave merchants truckling to Thorolf these past years—and it took a woman to handle him right proper. Horsewhipped him, she did! You should have seen him hopping! He was running for his horse, but the sight of a screaming woman with a whip panicked the beast. Yes, sir! Lamed himself trying to escape, did that horse."

The sweetmonger was nearby. "He speaks truth. I don't think Matilda ever hit Thorolf with her whip, but she came close. A while later, after Thorolf rode past my booth, she walked by headed in the direction of the tavern."

A cloth merchant spoke. "My wife and I have the next place over." He swept his hand to indicate the brightly-colored display. "About two hours after sunset, a horse in riding tack came to the paddock all lathered up. I recognized Matilda's mark on the saddle, so I let him in through the gate and unsaddled him."

The woman holding the cloth merchant's arm said "Matilda fell over our tent ropes, about the same time my husband was caring for the horse. I got her up, and tucked her away in her shed."

A babble of voices broke out, confirming Matilda's story in every detail and embroidering upon Thorolf's discomfiture. When there was no more information to be gleaned, Gervase and his men withdrew—this time to the center of the paddock, farther from listening ears.

"Men," Gervase began, "we've learned more than we expected. And right now, it doesn't seem to be worth much. We'll have to check the tavern to see if Matilda was there, but I expect she was. That leaves Ragnar Forkbeard as our chief suspect—at least Otkel seems to think so. He should know Thorolf's enemies.

"Dirk and I will go to the tavern. The rest of you, poke about and see what you can learn of Ragnar's activities. Try not to arouse his suspicions." Three troopers scattered, while the fourth remained with Matilda.

The tavern had a canvas fly, keeping sun and rain from a patch of ground the size of a large room. Rushes were strewn on the ground, and three-legged stools scattered about. The tables were sections cut from a very large tree, and smaller tree-chunks supplemented the stools. At one end an enclosed wagon was drawn up, with casks protruding from the rear and sausages and cheese hanging from the roof. Dozens of wooden mugs hung from pegs around the frame, and dimly within, bottles and loaves could be seen. The tavernkeeper was near the wagon. His wife and daughter moved about, delivering full mugs and collecting empty ones.

Gervase gave the tavernkeeper a silver penny. "A pint of bitter, bread and cheese. What will you have, Dirk?"

Dirk scratched absently at his stubble as he thought. "Ale, and sausage. Garlic sausage."

The tavernkeeper was named Tony, a tall, slat-thin man wearing shirt and breeches. Tucked into the band of his well-used apron was a large knife. He drew it, sliced cheese and sausage from his collection. He set mugs below the casks and pulled on the spigots: two streams arched forth, one dark and one golden. Gervase and Dirk took their mugs and drank in unison, sighed appreciation in unison.

"Ah," the bailiff said, wiping his mustache. "Murders are thirsty work."

"Tell me, Tony," he continued. "People talk at taverns. What have they been talking about?"

The tavernkeeper looked thoughtful, and drew himself a half-pint. "Well, most of yesterday people were talking of Thorolf's face-off with Ragnar. But a little before sundown, everybody was laughing over Matilda using a whip on him. I must say, the laughter seemed sincere—but it had a nervous edge."

"Matilda says she came here, but can't remember anything afterwards."

"Yea, that's the truth of it. She arrived very soon after the story did. Normally, she likes her pint of stout—but last night she was drinking ice wine. She definitely was in a hurry to get drunk. And half the merchants in the place were lined up to pay for her next drink. Maude tried to help her back to the paddock, but Matilda said she didn't need help. I'm surprised she was able to walk that far."

"She didn't make it all the way," the bailiff said. Tony nodded.

Two men, drovers by the look of them, came up to the wagon. "Ale!" they said. The tavernkeeper was silent a moment as he drew it.

"I didn't realize quite how much the merchants disliked Thorolf," Tony continued as the drovers seated themselves where they could look out over the crowd. "There was grumbling, especially when they were in their cups. But last night, they were toasting his downfall."

"Who were the merchants doing the toasting? Who was buying the drinks?"

"Mostly the toasts came from local merchants, and traders from the North. The carters were buying a lot of the drinks, but I think that was because Matilda is a horse person rather than because of Thorolf. I don't doubt most of them have wanted to take whip to the occasional rich man themselves.

"Then too, there was a lot of sympathy for Matilda. More than once, I heard people say something terrible would happen to her for this—that a man like Thorolf lost all his power if he let this sort of thing pass."

"They were right, too," Gervase said. "For Matilda, Thorolf's death is probably the best thing that could have happened. She'd be my chief suspect, if she hadn't had a hundred witnesses helping her get drunk at the time Thorolf was killed."

A woman arrived with a pail. Tony filled it with bitter, and gave her the cheese she pointed at, put her coin in his pouch, and watched her disappear into the confusion of the fair. "She's not out of the woods yet," he mused. "Who knows what Thorolf's men will do?"

A burly Northman came up, wearing a wool tunic and breeches. With him was a small southerner in doublet and hose. They paid for their ale and sausage, then the ill-assorted pair went to a table well away from the others and huddled over it, talking and eating. A family bought bread and bitter.

Tony's wife, Maude, came up to the trio. "You can talk later, Tony. There are people headed our way." She poured ale, grabbed a loaf of bread, and headed back into the crowd already there.

"It's coming on noon. As Maude says, if you still have questions we'll have to talk later." Tony turned to his customers. There were half a dozen, clamoring for ale and bitter, bread and cheese and sausage, apples—his entire stock. Maude and Tony wove an intricate dance around the kegs, pouring ale without getting in each other's way.

"I'd say it's time for us to get to work, too," Gervase said to Dirk. They parted. Dirk went to join two drovers as unshaven as himself, while Gervase sat at a table with a prosperous-appearing Northman. He nursed his ale and cheese in silence.

A discussion grew at Dirk's table, became louder and more heated. "Of course Matilda killed Thorolf—her, or a friend of hers! It was the only sensible thing to do!" Dirk's voice rose drunkenly. The drovers disagreed, loudly and at length.

Gervase thought that was one of the finest openings Dirk had ever manufactured for him. He turned to his companion. "Those two have the right of it," he said. "Matilda? Ha! The whole thing started when Thorolf was fool enough to threaten Ragnar Forkbeard. Anybody knows a man like Ragnar wouldn't allow that without taking action."

The Northman's teeth flashed. "Let me tell you about Ragnar, friend."

Chapter 4
Monday: Startling News

With the smell of smoke and breakfast, the crackle of fire, birdsong, sleepy voices in the distance, and daylight beginning to glow through the canvas roof of the booth, Ragnar came slowly to wakefulness. He lay in warmth between his bearskins, eyes closed, listening to the breathing and the snores of his crew.

But it was the first day of the fair—no time for sleep. He rose, scrabbled his feet into sandals, wriggled into a work tunic, and buckled on his belt with its sword, dagger, and pouch. Shuffling, not fully awake, he threaded his way to the door. Men were everywhere, sleeping on the benches and the floor, covered with blankets, furs, and cloaks. Some were beginning to stir.

Outside, all was misty. Some of the nearer booths and tents were pale areas of color, fading in the distance into grayness. Ragnar shivered from the chill, picked up his pace, and went rapidly to Gunnar's fire behind the booths. Knute was already there, helping Gunnar, and studying the way he controlled the fire under the cauldron.

Gunnar knew his leader. As soon as Ragnar appeared, he ladled out a soapstone bowl of hot broth, and handed it to him. Silently Ragnar took it, sat on a log, and began to sip. Silently Gunnar tore off a huge piece of barley bread, which Ragnar dipped in the broth.

"I butchered the buck, then threw the leavings in the river after most people were asleep," Gunnar said quietly, after some while. "He's in the other cauldron, simmering. I'll buy onions and barley from one of the merchants once the fair gets going, and it should be ready a little after noon."

"Ah," Ragnar smiled. "Be sure to use lots of sage. I like sage." He bit off another chunk of bread, chewed. "What do you think of yesterday?"

Gunnar considered the question. "Thorolf isn't our problem. His world is going too well. But we'd better watch out for Otkel. He looks restless from being in Thorolf's shadow."

"Is that just an opinion, or is it one of your prophecies? You know it's hard for you to keep a level head around Otkel."

"I kept my head when he tried to take it off me."

"That *is* a hard thing to forget, or forgive. I would have helped you, but I was busy with Thorolf at the time."

Gunnar shrugged, made a dismissive gesture. "It just feels like an opinion to me. But it'd match up with Otkel's past deeds."

Knute had heard the stories, growing up, of the famous battle between Snorri's faction and Thorolf's faction. Now it looked like he might be caught up in its aftermath. *Be silent. Listen.* Those were his father's words, and they seemed very appropriate for a time like this.

Men were drifting up to the fire now, holding out their bowls to Gunnar. Slowly, Northmen came to rest on the seating logs. Disheveled from sleep, surrounded by fog, they were a gloomy crew; but the hot food helped cheer them up.

One, red-eyed and nursing a hangover, spoke. "I drank too much. There are trolls in my head, with hammers, trying to get out. But the party was worth it!"

Several of his comrades, some in better condition and others in worse, agreed. "Aye!" "Tony has good ale!" "Thorolf horsewhipped! I haven't laughed so hard in ages!"

Heads picked up all around the circle, and eyes focussed on the speaker. "Thorolf horsewhipped?" Ragnar asked. "This is news to me!" A mutter of assent rose.

Slowly at first, then words tumbling over one another, the men who'd been at the tavern told the tale of Thorolf's discomfiture. Spirits rose, and laughter long and loud.

Still quivering, Ragnar wiped his eyes. "And me at the abbey so I missed it all," he lamented. "I've never in my life so regretted going to church." And chuckling still, he walked off toward the river, to wash himself in water fresh from the North.

Ragnar pictured Thorolf's wooing in his mind's eye. Nobody at the tavern had been sure what Thorolf had done, but the results had certainly been spectacular. *Matilda, for Frey's sake!* Everybody knew Matilda was one of the gentlest women on Earth!

He knelt at the riverbank, and began to wash his head and shoulders. "BbbbbbBB!" he blew through his lips from the chill. *That's what you needed, Thorolf—a cold bath.*

Gallantly speak, and presents bring
When wishing to win a woman's love.
Praise the beauty of the maiden:
Courting well will conquer.

When he returned, cheeks glowing from the spring-cold water, the fog had begun to lift and the men were thoroughly awake. Ragnar set them to work. "Get those display tables set up! Knute, pick a nice sampling of merchandise. Put it on display when the tables are ready! Atli, stand watch!" Two booths down, Olaf was preparing his display furniture. The furs and cloth would stay in his booth until the fog lifted completely.

Ragnar went inside to dress in clothes befitting a master merchant. First he put on bright breeches and soft elkhide boots, then a damask tunic trimmed with fur. He slipped on silver arm-rings, then pinned on a short cloak with a massive silver brooch. His belt had a buckle carved of moose antler, and a dagger with staghorn handle of his own making. His shortsword had been made by James Smith, of iron he himself had supplied. Finally he combed his hair and plaited his beard neatly.

He was touching up the display tables as the fair began coming to life. There was a hubbub down the way, a number of merchants gathered together, then one of his men, Atli's brother Ari, broke from the group and came running back to the booth.

"A rider just got here! He says Thorolf is dead, on the road to Northlanding!"

Ragnar carefully adjusted the position of an inlaid dagger before he looked up. "It would seem this fair has not been one of Thorolf's luckier ventures.

"Ari, you have sharp ears. Your brother Atli has good eyes. Take horses, and the two of you see what is happening. I want to know what the bailiff is doing, I want to know what Thorolf's men are doing. If you find something I should hear about, one of you should come back—but leave the other behind, to keep watch. Now off with you!"

He turned. "Olaf! Important news!" he called, and motioned. Olaf left his men to set out the furs, and came over. A southerner rode up to them—Ragnar recognized him as a wine merchant—and dismounted. "Thorolf is dead!" the merchant told them.

Olaf's eyes widened. "I've just been told," Ragnar said. "Are you the rider that brought the news? What happened?"

"I stayed the night in Northlanding, and started for the fair at dawn. Right off I met a runner, who said Thorolf was dead and he was going for the bailiff. Thorolf's body was just the Northlanding side of the abbey road. Benedict was there, watching over Thorolf's corpse. It looked to be an arrow that did Thorolf in."

"The trolls take Thorolf!" Olaf exclaimed. "We had to face him down yesterday. Now that somebody's put an arrow in him, everybody will remember that and come asking us questions."

"That's why I'm warning you," the man said. "We merchants have to stick together. Thorolf was leeching off us for too long as it was—I'd hate to see him take one of us with him into death."

The southerner mounted, wheeled his horse. "I have to get back to my wares before my helpers drink all the stock." And he rode off toward the wine-merchants quarter.

Ragnar watched him thoughtfully. "He seems to think one of us did it. Let's hope not too many feel that way."

Olaf shrugged. "It's not worth worrying about. We've more than enough men to handle Otkel and the others if they make a fuss. And Thorolf was outlawed – who cares who kills him? It'll be a bother, but we're only here for a week."

"The baron cares. Why do you think that Southerner was talking about Thorolf taking companions onto his pyre?" Ragnar saw Olaf still didn't understand.

"You've mostly traded to the east, where customs are more reasonable. The laws are different here. Except for self-defense, you've got to be some kind of lawman or soldier before you're allowed to kill people. Do it yourself, and they'll hang you. It's called justice."

Olaf was outraged. "That's terrible! Thorolf killed Snorri Crow, right?"

"I was there when it happened."

"The judges at the Althing pronounced full outlawry on him for the killing?"

"*Many* of us were there when that happened."

"And if we caught him in Surtsheim district, we could legally kill him?"

"If I caught him there, I'd have done it myself. But he left too rapidly."

"Now I come a few days downriver, and if I kill Thorolf some lousy English king who's never heard of me, or Thorolf, or Snorri for that matter, is going to have his sheriff or bailiff or somebody hang me for it?"

"I think this king is from the French branch of the ruling family, but you seem to have a fair grasp on the matter."

Olaf subsided into mutters and grumbles. "Damn if I'd want to have a king like that around. If the people who have to live with Thorolf decide the world would be better without him, who needs some stranger second-guessing us? Does he think he has a monopoly on justice, like the Miklagarders have on silk?"

Ragnar shrugged. "The customs are familiar at home, but you can't be a trader there. How much iron could I sell in Surtsheim? How much brocade could you sell in Miklagard? English money may have the face of their king on it, but melt it down to silver and it makes as good an arm-ring as any other silver. Anyway, the bailiff wouldn't act without evidence, and I don't think he has any pointing to us. But Thorolf's troubles started with us, and we may hear from Otkel about it yet. He's not the sort to worry about proof.

"They'll want a funeral, and it will take them all day to arrange one. We should try to get in as much trade as we can today, because tomorrow might be—interesting." Ragnar stroked his beard. "I think from now on, we'd better travel about in groups.

"And now—yes, good sir?" Ragnar turned to his wares, and the townsman examining one of his inlaid daggers. The customer looked modestly prosperous. "Finest iron, from Surtsheim," he assured the man. "I smelted it myself. Surtsheim iron is tougher than most."

"This is the kind of knife I want," the man said, "but maybe a bit smaller. It's a gift for my son."

Ragnar reached beneath the display, lifted a small chest onto a side table. "I have quite a few more." He searched about in the chest, pulled out a smaller knife decorated with niello, showed it proudly. "Two shillings, and worth every penny of it."

"That's a lot for a knife."

"Mainly, I sell iron," Ragnar admitted. "And a shipload of iron is heavy. So everything else I bring has to be worth a lot for what it weighs. I haven't got the freeboard to carry cheap knives. But Surtsheim is filled with iron-workers, who make handsome things. I always bring fine merchandise to sell.

"I *could* lower the price some. Wouldn't it be good for you and your son to have matching knives? If you bought both the small knife and the large, I could let you have the pair for three shilling sixpence. These two knives are special: I made the larger one, and my son Knute made the smaller. It would be appropriate for a matching pair, and I can drop the price for the appropriateness."

"...eight mansweights of iron *and* a mansweight of antler, then, for your glasswares and ten barrels of wine."

"Done!"

Ragnar and the sun-darkened river captain shook hands. "Gunnar!" Ragnar shouted back into the booth. "Two horns of ale!" Gunnar brought them out, smiling through his dark beard. Ragnar and the captain linked arms and drank to seal the bargain.

"You're tied up at the landing below the falls. My men will deliver the iron to your riverboat, and your men can deliver the glass and barrels to mine."

The captain looked over to the boats at the landing. "It's strange as strange. Two craft as unlike as ours, and both called riverboats."

"It's a different river above the Great Falls, even if it is the same water," Ragnar replied. "I have to be able to portage around rapids. I can imagine trundling a flat-bottom like your *Lady Jane* along a trail on rollers." Both men laughed immoderately, a gold earring twinkling and dancing below the southerner's ear.

"Knute!" Ragnar called out. "Get some pack horses from our dozen, and start carrying iron to Captain Henry's boat. He's bought eight mansweights."

"We've got mostly riding horses," Knute's reply floated back. "Benedict was supposed to be here with more pack horses by the time business started."

"He must have been held up," *And I hope the bailiff doesn't hold him up much longer,* Ragnar thought to himself. "Go rent pack horses from Matilda, then!"

"Right!" Knute grabbed two other men, and they trotted off in the direction of Matilda's paddock, vanishing between two tents across the way.

Soon they returned, each leading two horses. "Matilda had a two-man hangover," Knute said with just the right mixture of sympathy and smugness, "and her only one woman. That ice-wine will do it to you every time." They gathered up more Northmen, and headed off toward the boats and the iron.

"I'll go along with them," Captain Henry said. "With only six horses, they'll have to make at least two trips. The horses can carry glasswares as they return."

"It sounds reasonable to me," Ragnar noted. "But if I'm supplying horses for your loads, it's only fair you open up your stock of wine. My men are a thirsty lot, and they work better for a man who stands them drinks."

The captain punched Ragnar's shoulder, and drained his horn. "Me too—that's why I'm in the wine business. I'll try to leave them capable of walking back." Then he went toward the boats. Three of the men had boarded Ragnar's lead ship, and were lofting bars of iron over the gunwales into a pile on the beach below. The other six each held a horse's harness, well away from the flying objects and the noise.

Ragnar noticed movement out of the corner of his eye, and turned to see a well-to-do housewife examining his silver jewelry. She held out a length of handsome blue cloth, carried over her left forearm.

"I just bought this cloth two booths over, for to make a light cloak. Now I'll be wanting a clasp for it, and the gentleman told me you'd be having just what I needed."

"Why, that I do, goodwife!" Ragnar picked up a circle-brooch of silver, its pin decorated with a shining gray-black cabochon. "The latest fashion in Surtsheim district. See how the hematite stone sets off the blue of the cloth?" He held it near her elbow, where the fabric gathered into folds.

* * *

For the moment, Ragnar had no customers. He let his eyes roam across the fairgrounds: the bright tents and banners, the gaily-clad townsfolk, the peasants there to gape at things they couldn't afford—and maybe, to buy a small trinket if the price were right. The mood was brighter today: the merchants still were unobtrusively armed, but the crowd laughed and swirled with only the ever-present eating daggers and the occasional young bravo with a sword slapping against his thigh.

He looked over at Olaf's booth. The powerful figure was deep in conversation with a covey of fops, holding out brocade to them, stroking it as a mother would stroke her child. Ragnar could hear him speaking of the looms of far Miklagard, the long river journey, the storms of the big seas—and all so they, fortunate gentlemen, could see this finest of fabrics.

Now there's a man who loves his work, Ragnar thought. He turned back to the crowd, and saw Atli hurrying toward him, leading two horses.

He arrived panting. "Gunnar! Ale!" Ragnar called. "Sit down, Atli. Catch your breath." Gunnar brought a horn for Atli, who downed it gratefully and held it out for a refill. He took a sip, and sighed deeply.

"The bailiff is here at the fair, questioning Matilda," Atli began. He went on to recount the events of the morning. "They kept the crowd well away from Thorolf's body, so we couldn't hear anything. Otkel and the bailiff spoke for a long time, then Thorolf's men prepared to take his body away. Suddenly Otkel got off his horse, examined the body, and went over to the bailiff. They appeared to have some kind of argument. Otkel and the others left, and the bailiff dismissed us all.

"We followed the bailiff and his men directly to Matilda's. They aren't pushing the crowd quite as far back, there; my brother stayed to hear what he could. His ears are sharper than mine. I brought the horses with me, to free him up."

Ragnar smiled.

> Guests should be cautious when they come to table,
> And sit in careful silence,
> Ears attentive, eyes alert:
> Thus they protect themselves.

"You and Ari have done well this morning. This situation could be dangerous for all of us, here under English law. The bailiff seems to be looking elsewhere, though I doubt Matilda is in danger. She had too many people watching her last night at the tavern. Otkel is probably our chief worry. We should know more of his actions.

"They'll be arranging Thorolf's pyre at the sacred grove. It's been some time since you last sacrificed—perhaps this reminder of death in a foreign land might lead you to seek the favor of the gods?"

Ragnar reached to his neck for a leather thong, and pulled a silver Thor's Hammer from beneath his tunic. He placed it around Atli's neck. "Take this: good service demands good reward. There'll be a hammer for Ari, too. Go now, and see what Otkel and the rest of the funeral party are up to."

As Atli left, Benedict arrived with the packhorses and his men. There was a great crowd swirling about them, because everybody knew they had found the body. They were checking with him before they headed for the paddock. Ragnar wanted very much to follow and hear Benedict's tale. But he saw one of the local ironworkers, a steady customer, heading his way. An urchin whose looks he misliked was eyeing some of his more portable wares. And off in the distance Knute and the others were coming back from carrying iron to Captain Henry's boat. They seemed very jolly. The captain must have wined them well.

Too many things were happening at once. The muscles in his jaw knotted and his forked beard quivered as he tried to attend to them all, and failed. Then his world simplified – the customer had arrived. *Let the others talk to Benedict, then. He'll still be around later.*

"Good day, Ragnar! How was your voyage down to the fair?" said the ironworker.

"Excellent as always, my friend. The river flows rapidly and deep in the springtime. But I'd hate to row back upstream with a heavy cargo. Would you know anybody who might like to take some iron off my hands?"

Ragnar and the ironworker were concluding their sale. Ragnar had his scale out, was weighing silver offered in payment.

"Your bar is several ounces heavier than we agreed upon," he said. "I'll have to pay back the difference." He pulled a plain silver arm-ring off, hefted it, then straightened out a section. His small hatchet flashed down on a cutting-block; he weighed the piece, then added several small coins from his pouch until the scales balanced. He pushed the silver across to his customer.

Ragnar took tongs from beneath the table, twisted the end of the remaining arm-ring so the sharp edges couldn't catch the cloth. He put the ring back on.

"Knute!" he cried. "We've another three mansweights of iron to deliver, to Northlanding this time."

"I've sent several men to take the rented horses back. Now that Benedict's here, we have enough horses ourselves. I'll get right to it." Knute began gathering men from the crowd around Benedict, to the accompaniment of muffled grumbling.

Olaf's laughter rose. "You've been twice-told about Thorolf, and Benedict did a wonderful job describing Father Hugh being dragged through the bushes behind his donkey. Would *you* like to be dragged through the bushes behind a donkey? I could help Knute arrange it. Don't be so lazy, even if there isn't a promise of wine at the end of this trip."

Suddenly Knute had all the men he needed.

Ragnar, Olaf, and Benedict were in Ragnar's booth, in earnest discussion with Ari, who was saying, "The bailiff seemed to accept Matilda's story. But she was very upset, more than you'd expect from a woman who's just been cleared of suspicion. She may have cared more for Thorolf than she's willing to admit even to herself."

"He must have had some reason to romance her," Ragnar agreed. "And their last parting wasn't on the best of terms. Sometimes the gravest hurt is the one you do yourself."

"Somebody should keep an eye on her," Olaf added. "Whatever she had with Thorolf, she's earned trouble with Otkel. There are thirty of us. We're safe, as long as we stay in groups. There's just one of her."

One of the horsemen came in. "I just got back from Matilda's, and heard you were talking of her. She's in bad shape—just waved at us to let the horses into the paddock, then covered her eyes up again."

Benedict leaped to his feet. "I've had enough of deaths, enough of threats. Worry about Otkel yourselves. Here, by God, is something *I* can handle." He strode off. "Hob! Joseph!" he cried. "Stir yourself! We've horses to care for!" The three walked off in the direction of Matilda's paddock.

"I wonder if he realizes he just leapt from the cauldron into the fire," Olaf said dryly.

"Still, he has a point," Ragnar said as he rose. "Business goes on. I think it's time to sell more iron, and maybe some fabric and a bit of jewelry to go with the fabric."

There was a shriek outside, and Gunnar's voice raised in curses. The four Northmen ran out of the booth and around to the cooking area, loosening their weapons as they went. They found Gunnar by his cauldron, enormous spoon in one hand and a grimly satisfied smile on his face.

"Some scruffy Englishman was snooping around the back of your booth," he told Ragnar. "He was so busy eavesdropping he didn't notice me. I got him right on the cheek with boiling stew. He headed off into the crowd as if there were a Northman after him." Gunnar pointed with his spoon.

"He was probably just a beggar," Ragnar said. "I think your generosity in giving food to a beggar is very commendable." They all had a good laugh, then Ragnar and Olaf went back to their sales tables and took them over from their assistants.

Ragnar looked over the crowd with suspicious eyes. It was as brightly-colored as ever, moving ceaselessly to and fro, but he looked for stillness, lack of color. That fellow over there, at the potter's—he wasn't really interested in the crock he was examining. And Ragnar's booth was well within his range of vision.

As Ragnar watched, the potter spoke to the man. Ragnar knew without hearing what the two were saying: "Pardon, friend, is there anything I might interest you in?" "Just looking, just looking." Shortly the man moved on to the next merchant. Again, Ragnar's booth was well within his view.

One of the neighboring merchants, a cutler who specialized in Surtsheim iron, came by carrying bread, cheese, and a bucket of ale from the tavern. He hailed Ragnar in a friendly manner. "There certainly have been big happenings! All the merchants are buzzing over Thorolf's death. They can't get enough news. I've had several people asking me about that confrontation you had with Thorolf, yesterday. And I hear Matilda and the merchants near her paddock have been plagued with questions all day, too."

Ragnar gave a twisted smile. "It's a pity nobody saw Thorolf getting killed. That's the tale most of them would like to hear. But you make do with what's available."

"Too true, too true! Must be going, I'm carrying everybody's lunch. Good sales!" And the cutler strode merrily off, cheese bouncing in its net against his back.

Ragnar gestured to Gunnar to take the sales table, then went over to Olaf. "We're being watched by Englishmen. Best we do little and say less."

"What makes you think so?" Olaf asked.

"Well, there was Gunnar's eavesdropper. And then I saw this fellow over at the potter's...." Ragnar gestured in that direction, then realized the man was gone.

"Maybe we're all on edge and seeing things," Olaf said. "Or maybe the watchers have realized we've noticed them, and withdrawn. Either way, the answer's simple and just what it's been all day: we sell our wares, and don't go anywhere alone."

Olaf noticed a man in a tastefully gaudy herald's tabard, looking at his booth. He held up a bolt of brilliant red cloth. "Brightly-colored cloth, my lord, guaranteed not to fade! Just the thing for banners!"

The herald approached. "Red cloth doesn't hold its color well," he said dubiously.

"Ah, they've learned new dyes in Miklagard." Olaf pointed to pennants flying above his booth. "See those flags? I've flown them every fair for a year, and the red is still bright as new."

"The rope for that banner has turned pink," the herald pointed out. Ragnar knew from the flicker of expression on Olaf's face that there would be fresh ropes tomorrow.

Ragnar knew better than to discuss the virtues of cloth. He went back to his table, and soon found himself discussing the virtues of Surtsheim iron instead. Out of the corners of his eyes, he kept watch for watchers, but there no longer seemed to be any.

He'd about decided he'd been imagining things, and was showing iron bells to a jester, when he saw Gervase Rotour and Dirk Cachepol headed his way. They were accompanied by four men.

One of the men seemed to have a scalded cheek, and the collar of his tunic was stained with food. Another was the fellow who'd been at the potter's.

Chapter 5
Monday: Plain Speech

"This is not a good time or place," Ragnar told the jester. "Go, now—swiftly." Ragnar flashed a sidelong glance in the direction of the approaching bailiff.

There was a brief flash of incomprehension on the jester's brow, which did not fit well with the image of the knowing gleeman. Then the eyes in his homely-handsome face moved to follow Ragnar's gaze. Bards, jesters, and gleemen have an instant understanding of lawmen in all their manifestations. He gave Ragnar a sympathetic smile, and cartwheeled off to the sound of jingling brass bells.

Ragnar gathered his dignity about him, tried to settle his shrinking stomach, and sat on the chair just outside the door of his booth. It had been expensive, richly carved with a seat of tooled leather, but it had proven its worth many times over. A master merchant is more impressive in a chair befitting his status. An impressive merchant commands better prices. He adjusted the folds in his tunic, and then the bailiff and his men arrived.

Gervase Rotour was dark where Ragnar was ruddy. His clothes were plain, but of Miklagard cloth, and while Ragnar wore many rings and arm-rings of silver, Gervase wore a few massive rings and brooches of dulled gold. His hood had a long liripipe behind, which he tucked up into his belt. The tip hung solidly enough to indicate considerable weight. Was it money, Ragnar wondered, or an unobtrusive truncheon? Or both?

"Good day, Master Ragnar."

"Good day, Lord Bailiff," Ragnar replied. "I've been wondering if you might not pay me a call. Will you have a seat?" He gestured to the stool beside him, also carved, but not as well, and without a back.

Gervase sat down with a faint smile and a nod. His troopers unobtrusively surrounded them. Ragnar noticed more and more Northmen idly standing nearby. Olaf and the others were paying attention.

Gervase sighed, acknowledging the deadlock of forces. "I speak plainly. One of our richest local merchants is dead, killed from ambush on the road. There could be a great deal of trouble if his slayer is not found immediately.

"Thorolf Pike was seen arguing with you yesterday. Furthermore, you are from Surtsheim. It is no secret that he was outlawed there for the killing of Snorri Crow—and that you were one of Snorri's men. There are other evidences that suggest you may have been involved in Thorolf's killing, which I should like to give you a chance to explain."

"Bailiff," Ragnar spread his hands, "my conscience is quite clean in this matter. I'm sure I can give satisfactory answers to any questions you may care to ask."

"Hm," Gervase said, and was silent for a moment. "You were seen going toward Northlanding early in the afternoon, only a few hours after the argument. You returned after dark. And it is said you visited the abbey. Thorolf was killed just beyond the abbey road, shortly after sundown. You seem to have been very close to the scene of the crime, at the proper time of day."

"I visited the abbey, that is true, and stayed for Vespers. Darkness came on somewhat more rapidly than I had expected, which slowed my return to the fair."

"You were armed quite well when you rode out—sword, and a bow. Thorolf was killed by an arrow. Would those be your arrows, inside the door to your booth?" Gervase motioned, and one of his men went to get the quiver. One of Ragnar's men accompanied the bailiff's man.

Gervase took one of Ragnar's arrows, and the arrow which had killed Thorolf. He placed them side by side, and spent a long time comparing them.

"These arrows are very similar," the bailiff said at last. "Similar fletching, similar nocks, similar arrowheads. Why, both your arrowhead and the head of the arrow that killed Thorolf bear your mark. I should very much like to know how an arrowhead bearing your mark came to be found in Thorolf's body, hm?"

Ragnar smiled. *At least this is an easy question,* he thought, then whistled. "Gunnar! My small chest—you know the one I mean." Gunnar went into the booth and returned shortly, carrying a small but heavy iron-bound chest.

Ragnar opened it, revealing hundreds of arrowheads like the two the bailiff had been comparing. "I deal in ironwares, and have sold thousands of arrowheads here over the years. These were made in my own shops, and I'm proud enough of them to have signed them. Anybody could use one—why, the Master of the baronial archers was here just this morning and bought two hundred.

"Examine the arrows more closely. Mine has a pine shaft. The arrow that killed Thorolf has a shaft of maple. There are few maples in Surtsheim district, but many pines, so most Northmen use pine. Furthermore, the places where Thorolf's arrow-shaft was scraped are not the places I put my identifying marks. Your evidence suggests that Thorolf was killed by a resident of Northlanding, or a visitor from the south. As for my going armed, Benedict told me there were rumors of bandits."

"The cloak spread behind your booth has a bloodstain on it."

Sweat trickled down Ragnar's back. "I carelessly went hunting in it. That's the blood of an animal. In any case, what does this have to do with Thorolf? Benedict tells me the body was undisturbed. How, then, could bloodstains matter?"

"Certain of your men have been observed behaving in a furtive manner."

"Many merchants have this trait."

"This man is your cook."

"Gunnar isn't furtive. Could your trooper—the one with the scalded cheek—be trying to convince you that Gunnar crept up on him? Gunnar says the trooper was simply too busy eavesdropping to notice."

Gervase looked at the trooper in question, and raised one brow. "Hm."

Ragnar was silent a long moment then, fingers stroking his beard, twisting the sweat from its braided tips. At last he spoke. "Bailiff, Gunnar is a strange man. He was wounded in the head, from behind, in the battle six years ago when Snorri Crow was killed. Since then, he rarely sleeps. Most of the time he is normal—but occasionally he dreams, even while awake and moving about. Some of those dreams have proven prophetic.

"But if he were to kill somebody, it would be Otkel rather than Thorolf. Otkel is the one that struck him from behind. I was there when it happened. I tell you truth: you can safely forget Gunnar in searching for Thorolf's slayer."

Gervase was silent. Ragnar took this to signify thought. "Bailiff, plain speech deserves plain reply.

"I and most of my men had given our allegiance to Snorri rather than Thorolf in the matter that led to Snorri's death and Thorolf's outlawry. I myself killed two of Thorolf's men in the battle that followed, and Thorolf killed my foster-brother. Further, yesterday Thorolf was pressuring us to trade with him. This would have cost us all a great deal of profit from this trip. None of us are sad that he has been killed.

"However, it is our law that when we kill a man, we must announce it and submit the matter to the judgement of the community at the yearly Althing if summoned. Otherwise we would be guilty of the serious crime of secret murder. None of my men or Olaf's has said he killed Thorolf. While they might not tell you English, Thorolf was a Northman. If his killer were one of us, he'd announce it among us. Certainly he wouldn't fear the consequences, for Thorolf was outlawed and it's no crime to kill an outlaw. You must seek elsewhere for your killer."

Ragnar rose, and the bailiff stood with him. They clasped hands in farewell, then Ragnar spoke. "Otkel's brother-in-law died by secret murder. With legal wiles, Otkel wrested control of the steading away from his own sister. Thorolf had accumulated many riches. And Otkel is famous for his skill with weapons that strike at a distance."

With that they parted. Ragnar heaved a great sigh of relief. He made the sign of Thor's Hammer, then the sign of the Cross. "Thor be with me, Christ be with me," he murmured under his breath. He lifted his arms to ventilate his armpits a bit.

There came a green smell all about him, pungent of autumn herbs. Ragnar turned, to see James Smith.

"He looked to be grilling you pretty hard," James said. "But at least he went away in the end."

Ragnar fanned himself. "That was a tricky interview: he was giving me a chance to convince him I didn't kill Thorolf. I hope I *did* convince him—but let me tell you, I am sweating." He punched James lightly on the shoulder. "I'm glad you're here—after the bailiff, a friendly face is a sight for sore eyes.

And you're good for the nostrils, too. You certainly smell better than I must, after that conversation!"

James laughed. "I suffered for my smell, just as you suffered for yours. I was coming down with a rash, so I went to the abbey and begged some of Abbess Margaret's herb unguent from Father Hugh."

"Well, it's a welcome change," Ragnar said. "One of those troopers was wearing the worst bear-grease burn ointment I've ever smelled. He was skulking about earlier, and Gunnar scalded him with hot stew."

"Stew? That's an unlikely weapon."

"Oh, it's harmless when used properly. In fact, it should be ready by now. Would you care to join us in our meal? Then we can get back to the serious business of ironmongering." The two walked together toward the cauldron behind the booths. There was a mouth-watering aroma of meat and sage and onions.

Gunnar handed them bowls, bread and ale. A place was made for them. They sat, and ate, among peace and quiet conversation.

Two others were walking: Gervase Rotour and Dirk Cachepol. They sought solitude on the river road upstream of the fairgrounds.

"I don't like it, Dirk. Ragnar had excellent answers to all of our questions. And we'll have to consider Otkel a suspect, if what Ragnar said is true. I have little doubt it is. Ragnar has a good reputation for truth-telling. But there's something nagging me."

"He's a merchant, m'lud," Dirk said. "Makes him confident as the only rooster in the henyard when it comes to crossing tongues. You don't like confident suspects."

"And an honest merchant at that, which makes him doubly dangerous. We listened to what he said, which made perfect sense. And I'm sure it was the absolute truth. But was it the whole truth?"

"M'lud?"

"You know, he cleared all his men. But he never once said that *he himself* didn't kill Thorolf."

"You never asked him."

Chapter 6
Monday: Readying the Pyre

Otkel mounted up and waved his Northmen—by Odin, *his* Northmen—forward. The man riding the team-horse clucked and slapped it gently, and the ceremonial wagon lurched into motion.

Otkel was in the trailing group of horsemen. He cantered forward, conscious that people were watching, to the head of the band.

The bailiff had taken Thorolf's pouch of silver, and Otkel was certain it would never return. And now there was this trooper trailing along. *'Help him however you can', HA! A Welshman? The fellow had to be a spy.*

Otkel fumed, while his face remained solemn. The wagon creaked behind him, and there was the comforting presence of his men. The morning sun was well up and the day was warming. It would have been cooler without his bear-fur cape. He began to sweat, but he kept the cape. Thorolf deserved a well-dressed escort for his last ride here on Midgard.

There were people on the road who gave them a respectful right-of-way. Otkel's vision was keen. In the distance he could see oncomers as they sighted his band. They would scratch their heads and gesture to one another. Then somebody – there always seemed to be somebody—would come up. They would talk together, and point. Their eyes would widen, and they would move to the far side of the road.

Sometimes there would be a flash of smile, vanishing almost before it began. Otkel marked those faces in his memory.

There was a side road some distance beyond the abbey road, less used than this merchants' thoroughfare, leading down an arched avenue of elms. The band of Northmen turned down it. Immediately the sound of the horses' hooves and the rattle of the wagon-wheels quieted. The main road had been beaten down, the dirt washed away by the rains, the rocks left behind. Here, the grasses still held sway and the rocks were few.

They traveled in silence below the elms. It was like riding the length of an enormous longhouse. Rays of light lanced through leaf-windows into the dimness beneath. Slowly the forest changed. Graceful elm gave way to gnarly oak, and the land began to rise. Ahead, through the trees, was a handsome hall shining in the sun.

The road came into a large clearing with two hills. One hill had a building at its top, three times as tall as a man and covered with rounded shingles so it seemed scaled like an ancient dragon. It was small for a temple, but well-built. Near the temple was a great oak with golden torcs and silver arm-rings, bronze helmets and other sacrifices hanging from its branches. Much of the clearing around and beyond this hill was devoted to a temple farm and its buildings, all handsomely painted.

The other hill was bare, with a circle of burnt stones at its summit.

When they left the shelter of the trees, they saw tall wooden poles set into the ground close beside the trail. Some were plain and some carved with faces. Otkel and the others dismounted there, and gave their horses into the care of a temple servant. Leif stayed with the wagon as the others went forward. His left hand held the reins of the lead horse, while his right hand wrapped about his crucifix. His face was still, and closed.

There were two pillars side by side, larger than the others. One bore a face with an eyepatch, the other the image of a bearded man with a hammer held beneath his chin. Otkel prostrated himself before the first. "Allfather Odin, I come bearing the body of your servant Thorolf, killed by shameful hidden ambush. Tonight there will be a mighty pyre, and many sacrifices; tomorrow, vengeance. We pray you: smile upon the pyre, smile upon the vengeance."

The Northmen lay in silence before the pillars, some praying to Odin and others to Thor. A breeze sprang up, rattling in the oak-leaves. A shadow flickered over them, and there was the sound of wings. Otkel looked up.

One post, apart from the others, had a face with lines stitched across its mouth: Loki, a very treacherous god. A raven had landed on it, and was regarding them. As the Northmen began to move, to look toward it, it cawed loudly and took off, slow wingbeats swirling the air. It flew to the edge of the wood and joined a flock of ravens perched in a tree.

Otkel did not like the looks of that. Ravens often carried messages. *The bird of Odin, landing on the image of Loki? It doesn't seem likely I'll be able to rely on the favor of the gods in this matter.*

But he stood, and spoke. "We've been given an omen, men, and it seems very clear to me. The bird of Odin, battle-crow, bird of death, landed by us then took off. Death is with us for just a short while, and Odin's favor will be fleeting also.

"Then the bird of death joined with a flock—and who among you can tell me which one it was? Soon the killer will leave, join with others of his kind. Then we'll never be able to pick him out.

"The raven landed on Loki's post: Loki, god of craft and slyness. That means we'll need craftiness.

"Put them together. The killer is here at the fair, and we have to find him before everybody leaves at the end of the week. If we're clever, Odin will smile upon our vengeance—but we must act rapidly."

They stood, brushing twigs and leaf-fragments from their fine clothing. Otkel strode decisively over to the wagon, followed by the others. Leif quickly crossed himself, and stood alertly with the reins. They continued down the path on foot, Otkel leading, Leif guiding the horses, and the others forming a guard of honor about the wagon.

The path led past the temple and the sacrificial oak, on to the knoll topped with stones. As they approached the oak, a gray-robed priest carrying a rune-carved spear stepped forth to block their way. He grounded the butt of the spear firmly on the bare earth of the path. "Who walks the ways of the dead?" he asked.

"Thorolf Pike, and his men," Otkel replied.

"Thorolf is dead, that I can see. Where are your wounds, to give you the right to walk here?"

Otkel stepped forward, and bared his arm. The priest slashed it with his shining spear-head. A thin line of red droplets sprang out on Otkel's forearm, and a rivulet of blood formed. Otkel held his arm out, let the blood fall on the oak-roots, then stepped past the priest and stood by the side of the path. The next man came to the priest, and gave him his arm.

Leif was last, and he didn't present his arm to the priest. "I am a Christian now, and must not shed blood sacrifice to Odin."

"Then you cannot pass." The priest spread his feet and planted the butt of his spear firmly on the ground. "We have spoken of this before, Leif." They stood confronting one another. The priest was tall and gaunt. His silver beard, shot with a memory of red, gleamed in the sun. Leif was short and stocky. Gray was just beginning to show in his hair.

"Thorolf was my friend," Leif said, "and Odin is Lord of poetry and mead as well as of battles and death." Leif took a mead-skin from his belt and drank, then poured a shining golden stream of honey-wine onto the tree's roots. "There is a poem in the holy book of Ecclesiastes:

> To every thing there is a season, and a time to every
>   purpose under heaven:
> A time to be born, and a time to die;
> A time to plant, and a time to pluck up that which is
>   planted;
> A time to kill, and a time to heal;
> A time to break down, and a time to build up;
> A time to weep, and a time to laugh;
> A time to mourn, and a time to dance.

"Thorolf was my friend," Leif said once more. "His time to die came. Now it is time to mourn, and perhaps it shall soon be time to kill. Your god and mine can agree on these things."

Shaking his head, the priest nevertheless stepped to one side. Leif joined the others. The path led down, then up again. Soon they were at the top of the burning-knoll. Wind blew gently about them, their cloaks of red and brown and blue flowing at their backs, the bear fur of Otkel's cloak rippling in the breeze. All around they could see treetops, and in the distance the walls and roofs of Northlanding.

At the foot of the hill were storage sheds of oak and ash and elm, stocked with dried wood for the pyre. It would be their last act as Thorolf's men to pile that wood for him, place him upon it, and set it alight. Then they would drink the funeral cup as the flames set Thorolf's spirit free.

They looked at the woodsheds below, and the bare hilltop; at the hill, and at each others' finery. They looked at their own clothing. Ceremony was over for a while, and it was time to haul wood. In their best tunics.

"Leif, you and Hermund and I will go back to Northlanding to get grave-goods for the pyre." Otkel swung his hand to indicate the rest of the men. "You build the pyre, and...."

"Just a moment there, Otkel," one of the men said. He was well-muscled, with battle scars and somewhat of a reputation as a berserk. "How come you always have other duties when there's heavy work to be done? Where were you last night, when the rest of us came back from a full day at the trade fair, and then had to spend hours sorting merchandise, hauling goods, and supervising the other workers? Where were you last week, when we were getting things ready for the fair?

"For that matter, you're getting a bit ahead of yourself ordering us around. We're free men, not thralls—we *choose* our leader. And we haven't chosen you, yet."

Otkel's mind dropped into a frozen calm, cold as the northern winter so recently past. He knew the men didn't especially like him, but they respected his cleverness. A challenge was bound to come. Handle it right, he'd be leader. Handle it wrong, an exile twice over. Now it was time.

He looked at the berserk before him. "People are very cautious around you, Starkad. You're a dangerous fighter with a dangerous temper. But if it comes down to that, I have as many dead enemies as you do.

"Remember, here in Northlanding we're not a war-band—we're traders. An English merchant isn't going to give you money because he fears you—not year after year. He's going to call in the bailiff, or hire guards, or worse.

"They give you money because they fear what might happen if they don't. You make an excellent consequence, standing behind the man doing the bargaining. But do you know how to let a merchant save his pride while giving you what you want? Do you know how to make the hint of violence do more than violence ever could? Do you fully understand what Thorolf and I were doing?

"I would make the threats. You would make the threats believable. Thorolf would restrain us, and the merchants would give the bargain to *him*. I'm going to have enough difficulty holding our deals together, myself. The rest of you would end up cooling your heels in a cell, or dead in an alley, if you tried.

"You, Starkad!" Otkel's forefinger stabbed toward him. "Back in Surtsheim you were a soldier. Here, you're a rich soldier. Hrapp! You tended other men's horses. Here, men make way for you in the streets. And you, Hallbjorn! On the docks of Lakesend you wore rags—here, the finest of linens!"

His eyes swept the men. "Look at you!" he cried. "The handsomest band of Northmen you're likely to see. Nobody had to give you those clothes for the funeral—you already had them. Thorolf and I did all the negotiating that made us rich. Now that Thorolf's dead, I'm the only one among us that's done it."

He turned, motioned Leif and Hermund to follow him. "Let's get Thorolf properly burned. We're going to have our hands full tomorrow, holding together the deals he made, and taking proper vengeance. But first things first."

He walked down the path. Leif and Hermund followed. For once, Otkel did not look back. He was quivering inside, but there was a melting warmth of satisfaction. *I do think I carried it off,* he thought to himself.

On the hilltop, the remaining Northmen began stripping down to their breeches, getting ready to carry firewood.

Otkel, Leif, and Hermund reclaimed their horses from the temple barn. The bailiff's man was talking quietly with the stableman in the horse-scented dimness within. The horses' heads came around and their ears pricked up as their masters entered.

As Otkel took the reins, the trooper headed toward his own horse. Otkel waved him off. "You needn't come with us. The men here will probably need you more. They've got a lot of ritual to get through, and it could be extremely helpful having somebody who's not involved, to take care of other matters."

They mounted, and walked the horses out along the path, toward the Northlanding road to the East. The Welshman stood in the stable entrance, looking alternately at Otkel's group and the Northmen on the burning-knoll.

Yes, help us in whatever ways you can, Otkel thought. *I hope they think of a few jobs for you to do. Interesting ones.*

"I'd think the temple servants could handle errands for the men building the pyre," Leif said. "Things could get complicated in Northlanding. Maybe we should have brought him."

"I don't like being followed about by lawmen," Otkel replied.

It was half an hour's easy ride to town—close enough to be convenient, far enough to spare the Bishop of Northlanding from a Norse temple on his doorstep. Conversation flickered and died, and they spent the latter part of the journey wrapped in silence, each with his own thoughts. Oak gave way to elm, elm to fields.

They came into the city at the western gate, their horses' hooves clattering on the cobblestones of the Sunset Road. Traffic was different here. On the fairgrounds road there had been merchants, buyers, people headed for the fair. Here, people rode sleeker horses or none at all, and Otkel recognized fewer faces.

The Angelus bell rang for noon as they were passing the cathedral, a deep resonant sound. Many of the people around them stopped for a brief moment of prayer. Out of the corner of his eye, Otkel saw Leif's lips moving in silent speech. *Angels and virgins, bah!* Otkel thought. *But that church has some nice treasures. One of these days, when I get tired of the merchant's life....*

But I don't think I'll take Leif along on the raid. So the day's only half-done? It's felt like forever.

They turned left, and headed north into the merchants' quarter. They met several groups of porters and carters, carrying merchandise to and from the fair. A train of horses was bringing bolts of cloth into Benedict's yard.

The gate was open at their warehouse, with several servants waiting by it. Nobody else was in the yard. When the overseer saw the Northmen, he seemed nervous.

"Well?" Otkel asked, as he dismounted and tossed the reins to a stablehand. "You're just standing around? Haven't you got merchandise to sort out inside? We were supposed to be getting iron, copper, wine, furs, and lots of seasoned oak timbers. And spices."

"Master, we've been waiting all morning ready for the shipments, just as you told us. But none have come."

"Hel take those merchants!" Otkel swore. "Do they think just because Thorolf is dead, their deals are dead also? They'll learn otherwise, tomorrow!" He snatched the axe from his shoulder and hurled it across the yard, where it struck deep into a post at chest-height. The post was heavily scarred from weapons practice, and it split apart from the blow.

Startled by Otkel's sudden motion, the horses reared up. The stableman fought them back under control. Otkel backhanded him. "Watch what you're doing more closely!" Then Otkel turned to the overseer.

"You have the list. Go to the fair, and talk to the merchants we have bargains with. Tell them I'll be speaking tomorrow with those that don't deliver today." And Otkel stalked off toward the house.

"I think Starkad is lucky he backed down," Leif murmured to Hermund as they followed.

They went in the warehouse through the main door to the yard. In the light seeping through the barred and shuttered windows they saw dim mounds of boxes, heaps of iron bars, and bundles of wool, flax, fur and cloth. The scent of pine tar was everywhere. Threading their way to the front, they climbed the staircase into the greathall.

Here above the street, away from prying eyes and reaching hands, the shutters were open and the windows flung wide. Fresh and fragrant rushes covered the floor, and all the metal was polished. The servants had worked at housekeeping for weeks, preparing for the trade fair. Thorolf dearly loved playing the open-handed host in his hall. Many merchants had shared his feast – and not a few gladly. The room smelled of springtime, but now Otkel would be host.

"We'll want his shield." Otkel pointed to where it hung on the wall behind the high-seat. "He was wearing his sword, and carrying his polearm, so they're already at the grove. Then, there's his drinking horn...." The Northmen set to work gathering valuables into a small pile in the center of the hall. Soon they'd gotten everything appropriate in sight.

"Leif, why don't you check the solar to see if there's anything there? Hermund and I will see what should be taken from Thorolf's room." The hall was most of upstairs, and the men slept on benches along the walls. At the south end was a solar, a small cheerful room with a stained-glass window, where Thorolf could discuss business in private. At the north end, a small room where Otkel slept, and a larger room where Thorolf had slept and kept his treasury.

Otkel and Hermund crossed the hall, opened the door, went in. There were oiled-parchment windows on two walls, and a silk hanging on a third. Thorolf's bed was piled high with rare and beautiful white bear furs, and one was on the floor. At the head of the bed was a massive log chest, wrapped with iron straps studded with many nails. It had three padlocks. Leaning in the corner were half-a-dozen different pole weapons.

Otkel went to the windows, swung them open to catch the breeze, then turned back to find Hermund stripping the furs from the bed. "I think Thorolf will rest more easily on these."

That is going to be my bed, and it is going to have white furs, Otkel thought. "I don't know as he'll need the warmth on his pyre."

He looked about. That wall-hanging was appliqued in elaborate Ringerike style, and Otkel detested Ringerike. "Look. That's his favorite hanging, and it's got wonderful decorations. It would make a handsome drapery on his pyre, for him to rest upon. Then there's the satin cushion in the solar for his head."

"You know, that does sound better. He was immensely proud of that hanging. How many times have we heard him tell guests how it was brought across the sea from old Norway?" Hermund dropped the furs back on the bed, and he and Otkel took the hanging down and folded it carefully.

"It seems to me," Otkel added, "that Thorolf will want to make a good display in Odin's halls. We'll burn several of his best tunics and such with him. And then there'll be the battles. Maybe we'd better take along a halberd for him, and an extra sword or two. You're a good halbardier—pick out the best we have."

Hermund went over to the pole-weapons, while Otkel opened Thorolf's clothes-chest and began taking out tunics. He found three keys also, and quietly slipped them in his pouch while Hermund's attention was on the weapons.

They took their choices out into the main hall, and found that Leif had already gotten the satin cushion, and a number of other things. It made a rich pile, and they looked at it in satisfaction.

"We couldn't do much better unless we brought him here, set him in his high-seat, and burned the warehouse down around him. But the fire wardens wouldn't like that." Otkel clapped his hands. "Let's get the servants to packing this."

Leif frowned. "There should be more silver."

"Silver is for the living. Thorolf will need weapons in Valhalla, for the battles, and clothing and some jewelry for the show. But with Odin as lord and ring-giver, what need will Thorolf have of more silver than he can wear?

"Besides, his treasure-chest is too heavy to move. The keys aren't in his clothes-chest. They could be in his pouch, but the bailiff has that. It'll take a while to get it open, time we don't have now.

"I have jewelry Thorolf gave me. We **all** have his ring-gifts. I say we each put the silver he's given us on his pyre, so he'll have testimony to his generosity in Odin's halls.

"Then, after the fair is over, after we've taken our vengeance on Thorolf's killer, we can have a smith in and get the treasure-chest opened. And I pledge to be as open-handed with those treasures as ever Thorolf was."

Otkel called the chief cook over. "You know how Thorolf had you preparing for a feast? We'll invite the people at his funeral to keep it. Start roasting the geese an hour before sunset, and the timing should be right."

Soon they were riding back to the grove, followed by pack horses laden with grave-goods. Their mood had lightened considerably. Leif felt better knowing Thorolf would have a pyre worthy of his status. Hermund was relieved to see Otkel turning into a decisive and capable leader. And Otkel was glad to see the men falling into line. *We'll show those merchants, tomorrow,* he thought.

As they entered the clearing, they saw another man dismounting by the god-posts. He wore a magnificent Thor's Hammer—they could see it even at this distance. He prostrated himself before the bearded figures.

As they rode past, they heard him saying, "Now I come to you with these offerings," as he placed bread, onions, meat and ice-wine before the gods. "I want you to send us merchants who have much silver, and will buy on our terms without being difficult." And again he prostrated himself.

"That looks like Atli, from back in Surtsheim," Leif noted. "He was just starting to grow his beard when we left. He seems to be rising in the world these past few years."

A sour look came over Otkel's face. "I don't like the company he keeps. Wasn't he with Ragnar yesterday?"

"That was yesterday," Hermund said. "And it may be important again tomorrow. But this is holy ground, and a time for memories of Thorolf's virtues and not others' faults." They passed on up the hill.

Chapter 7
Monday: Gifts to Odin, and to Men

Gods gleamed, in firelight and the rays of the setting sun slanting through the windows. Under their gaze, Otkel lit his oak-brand from the sacred flame in the longhouse. He carried the fire out the door—how it diminished in daylight!—and solemnly walked the path down one hill and up the other, joining the twelve men in a circle round Thorolf's pyre. Travelling sunwise he kindled their brands one by one from his own, then took his place at the head of the pyre.

Below, the woods had darkened. The day birds were singing their evening songs, while one early nighthawk darted through the air screaming his thin cry. The last rays of the sun shone upon Thorolf on his high bed. A heap of silver lay upon his chest, and swords were at his side. The hanging, draped over his pyre, blazed with color. Fantastic beasts writhed and twined and struggled in silence, a silence joined by Thorolf's men and by the small group of mourners off to one side.

The sun touched the earth. From the other hill, two priests sounded their lur-horns. Otkel thrust his firebrand into the pyre below Thorolf's head. "Now I give you to Odin," he proclaimed in a strong voice. The pyre, of oak and ash and elm, began to burn.

Flames spread as the other men also put their brands to the pyre. "Now we give you to Odin," they said in chorus. Leif was silent, but he thrust his firebrand forth with the others.

The sun went beyond the edge of the world. The fire grew. Slowly light shifted, until they were illuminated solely by the glow of Thorolf's pyre. Flames and smoke rose straight. The embroidered animals were gone now, the tunics lumps and flame-edged tatters, the pillow a hard black stone, Thorolf's body a charring stick-man purged of all Earthly seeming. His polearm and the halberd picked by Hermund stood sentinel, one on either side.

The iron-bound shaft of the halberd began to give, and it leaned slowly against the polearm. The polearm's shaft cracked, buckled, and broke. The iron heads fell onto the pyre and shook loose a shower of sparks rising to the heavens. A wind came up, fanning the flames, carrying the glittering smoke toward the longhouse of the gods on the other knoll.

Hermund laughed hugely. "Odin loves Thorolf! He sends a wind to carry him to Valhalla!" Over the crackle of the flames they could hear the wind rushing through the treetops below; then the wind died down.

Otkel turned to a tripod behind him, lifted a huge cup and held it high. "The cup of Bragi," he cried. "Let us drink of the funeral ale, in memory of our leader and in praise of the god to whom he has gone!" He brought it to his mouth, tilted, drank. Firelight gleamed from the golden figures, flickered deep in the blood-red garnets studded about the curve of the cup.

Otkel turned to Hermund at his left, handed him the cup. "To Thorolf, to Odin, and to vengeance." Hermund repeated his words, drank deeply. He passed the cup to the next man. "To Thorolf, to Odin, and to vengeance."

The cup traveled around the circle, came back to Otkel. He drained it, held it high. "To Thorolf, to Odin, and to vengeance!" he and all the men cried in one voice. Otkel placed the bragarfull cup back on its tripod, and stood before it, lit from behind by the pyre. He spread his arms for silence. He spoke.

"Thorolf was our leader. Powerful of spirit, an open-handed ring-giver, he was a man of many ventures. Friends looked to him for protection, enemies feared him, rich men worried when they heard of his approach. Such men seldom die in bed.

"Nor did Thorolf. He died wealthy, with strong followers to give him a worthy pyre. But he did not die in battle. By all accounts he never had a chance to face his foe. Nor has anybody come forth to claim his death. Death in combat is the due of the leader of warriors – it's shameful that Thorolf should die without the chance to battle against his nameless attacker.

"I curse whoever has shamed Thorolf, and call down the wrath of Odin upon him. Let Thorolf's true men discover who did such dishonor, and take vengeance. Let Odin guide us in this. And let us carry out Thorolf's plans and deeds as if he were still with us, rather than letting his actions be forgotten. No man can ask for a better monument.

"We, Thorolf's men, are left to do battle for him. We have drunk from the sacred cup. It's now time for us to swear the bragarfull oath. Here is the oath I propose:

"You have heard my curse, and my prayer. Now I swear to help fulfil them: to take vengeance for Thorolf's dishonor, and to keep his deeds alive." Otkel drew his sword, held it above the cup with its point to the heavens. The others drew their swords also, and joined him.

"So say we all!" every man cried, and many of them wept at the power of Otkel's words and for their lost leader.

They sheathed their swords in the dying firelight, and Otkel filled the cup again from a nearby keg. He turned to the other mourners, those not of Thorolf's band. They were a mixed crew: several small merchants, a crippled boy and his mother, Northmen, southerners. Rhys, the bailiff's man, was among them.

Otkel carried the cup over to them. "And what better way to keep Thorolf's memory alive than by honoring those who honor him? Come with us, back to his hall. There will be food and drink, and a bard. Thorolf was planning this celebration for weeks, and we shall keep it." He handed the cup to a gnarled old man, a local dealer in roots and herbs.

The man held the cup, looked over its rim at the flames of the pyre. "I remember Thorolf. When he came to town with you, and began asking local merchants for a share of their business, I thought him very hard to deal with, and gave him his share grudgingly.

"Then as I was returning from an herb-gathering trip, wild bandits came out of the wood. They robbed me, and set my wagon on fire. They were having sport with me when Thorolf came riding alone. He killed two of them, and chased the other three off; then he returned, bandaged me, and gave me all the goods he'd captured from the bandits."

He lowered his lips to the rim of the great cup, and drank. Firelight gleamed on his baldness, picked out his wrinkles. He raised his head again, and Otkel could see tears. "He saved my life. He was still hard to deal with – but he held by his deals, and took care of his own." He returned the cup to Otkel.

Now Otkel gave the cup to a southerner. "I too remember Thorolf." Memories flickered across his tanned face with the shifting light of the pyre. "I remember his hearth-fire. Two years ago a scow escaped from its moorings, and rammed my ship just off Northlanding. We foundered before we could reach the shore. Thorolf was passing by, with all of you. You threw out a line and pulled us into the shallows, then Thorolf set the bunch of you to salvaging the cargo while he took me and my crew back to his hall.

"He hosted us for a week, until matters could be settled. He bought my cargo. The two of you –" his eyes locked with Otkel's "—drove a harsh bargain for damaged goods, then more than made up for it by repairing my ship."

He raised the cup to his lips, gold and garnet in his earlobe echoing the gold and garnet of the cup. "I've drunk Thorolf's ale before. I'm proud to do so now, and saddened I'll no longer have the chance in the future." He drank.

He returned the cup to Otkel, who passed it among the rest, then took it back to its tripod.

"Thorolf's spirit has gone. Let us go to his hall, and honor his passing." He handed out torches to all, and they lit them from the dying pyre. They walked down the hill and into the night, Otkel in the lead, holding the torches high.

As they passed the horses, the crippled boy's mother lifted him onto his pony. "Thorolf saw Jem hobbling down the street with his crutch. He swept him up on his horse and rode off to Milltown, and bought him this pony from Matilda. Now Jem knows every street in Northlanding, and earns enough carrying messages to pay for the pony's upkeep, and warm clothing besides. Bless Thorolf for his gifts!" She embraced her child as he sat with four strong legs beneath him, and both of them wept.

The other horses, less placid, shied at the firebrands. Otkel reassured the mourners. "I'll send men to bring them to Northlanding. Come to the fountain square in the merchant's quarter at noon tomorrow." Holding their torches still, the mother leading the pony, they formed a small procession. As they entered the woods, the mosquitoes started to bite. People began to slap at them. It broke the solemn mood, as annoyance can.

People came together, talking quietly, in groups of two or three or four, and passed through the darkness of night up to the watchfires of Northlanding.

The western gate was closed. A watchman leaned from a crenel, his face lit from below by their torches and those on either side of the gate. "Who comes at night?" he asked with a voice worn featureless by repetition.

"The friends of Thorolf Pike, from his funeral pyre."

The watchman's face disappeared, and there was a rattling of chains from within. The massive gate swung open, and the procession walked through the gatehouse into the streets beyond. Behind, the gate squealed shut.

Once they heard the sounds of revelry from an enclosed yard, and there were a few windows still lit. Occasionally a shutter would open a crack and an eye peer out at their torches. But the town slept, and they met none but the night-watch until they came to their warehouse.

The upper windows were thrown open, and the shifting glow of a fire lit the hall within. A small group of men and women stood at the gate—Christian friends unwilling to go to the Sacred Grove even though it was well away from the watchful eyes of the Church. The servants were waiting. The gates flew wide as Otkel and the others approached. The two groups came together and embraced in mutual consolation. They went in, and up the stairs.

The servants had set out trestles while everybody was at the funeral, and there were many delicacies: jams and honey and sweet cakes of maple sugar, formed into figures; pots of butter and little loafs of white wheat-bread; last year's winter apples, preserved in the cool caves of the river-bluffs. Drinking-horns were scattered about, and an enormous horn at the head of the table. Great trenchers of barley bread rimmed the trestle board, and sweating cooks were bringing a huge roast up the stairs from the cook-house in the yard.

The guests scattered into the room and took seats on the benches around the trestles. Bursts of talk and of silence alternated. Then Otkel raised his hands. "Dear friends, we are here to celebrate Thorolf. Let's do so." He raised the horn from the head of the table, freshly filled to the brim, and drank until he was forced to quit for air. "Ah," he said, wiping his moustache, and handed the horn to Leif, still very full. Leif made a valiant attempt to drain it, but there was still ale left when he handed it on.

Otkel looked at Thorolf's high-seat. *Tomorrow,* he thought, and sat in his usual place on the bench next to it.

Servants moved about, carving meat and filling horns with ale. And now a bard sang in a clear voice, verses made that day in honor of Thorolf. There was a hush, then one of the Northmen who'd been at his horn quite seriously knocked over a bowl of apples. They went rolling across the table, thumping to the floor, accompanied by gales of mirth. At the foot of the table two Northmen wept. The bard began another poem.

Otkel sat in his chair next to the empty high-seat, and sipped his ale. He'd taken an extremely large drink, that first pull at his horn, and now of all times, his wits should not be dulled.

One of the servants set a pie before him. The odor of cinnamon was heavy in the air, and Otkel suddenly realized how hungry he was. He drew his dagger, cut a slice. Venison, apples, and spice complemented one another. He swallowed, took another bite. *I didn't know we had cinnamon in stock,* he thought. *I'll have to take a better inventory soon.*

Talk and song ebbed and flowed, growing freer as the people drank. Occasionally somebody would have a special story of Thorolf, and the room would hush as they told it.

One of Thorolf's men spoke. "Do you remember that merchant from Saint George? Proud as a peacock, and dressed like one, with six bodyguards in silk? Turned down Thorolf's invitation, he did. Claimed a pavilion from Saint George was better lodging than any greathall here in a howling wilderness whose only virtue was fur-bearing animals."

"Didn't he snub the Bishop, too?" another voice added.

"Well, Thorolf sent Otkel out. He got one of the fellow's cooks drunk, and found that the merchant was running short of absinthe. Nasty stuff, that. Thorolf doctored some absinthe up with a strong purgative—who can taste anything else beside the wormwood?—and stocked up all the wine merchants, with strict instructions.

"Next thing you know, here come two of the peacock's guards, off to get the best doctor in town. 'Our master has been taken ill!' they said. Well, he'd actually just had a drink of freshly-purchased absinthe. We took 'em with no trouble.

"We sent a litter to fetch the merchant 'to the doctor,' and as soon as he and the remaining guards were away from the camp, we took them, too. Hit 'em over the head, stripped 'em, and left 'em in the ditch. We were disguised, of course.

"Thorolf 'just happened by,' and took the victims off to his hall to recover. Six of us put on the guards' silk livery and broke the merchant's camp, and nobody looked twice at us.

"Thorolf gave the merchant his own bed, and treated him well in every way. He dressed all the guards in fine embroidered linen, and gave each of them a silver ring and a good sword. They looked like proper Northmen, almost. Meanwhile, he had the tent off at the dyers, being dyed green.

"When the merchant was back on his feet, he couldn't find words enough to praise Thorolf's hospitality. He asked if he could stay a bit longer, because he'd learned his entire camp had been stolen.

"Now, most of the fellow's merchandise was still back on his riverboat with his crew. We'd made a nice haul of his personal possessions, but he still had a lot left.

"So Thorolf explained that he had family coming from up North, and there wouldn't be room, but he had a fine pavilion in his warehouse. They dickered for hours, and Thorolf struck a very hard bargain with him. It cost that merchant a third of his goods for that tent.

"I wish I could have been there to hear him, when he had it pitched and learned he'd bought his own pavilion back—and dyed plain green at that, instead of a fancy yellow and blue like it was before! He raised a fuss, of course, but the bishop intervened and the peacock was sent packing. Thorolf and the bishop never got along as well as then, before or since."

The entire room rang with laughter. Boots stamped, and Northmen pounded on the table. The servants scurried about filling horns with ale, and the bard sang a ribald song, with many gestures, about the difficulties suffered by the nobles of Saint George when they tried to mix absinthe and lovemaking.

Otkel sat, listening to the tales of Thorolf's deeds and generosity. *Who will tell Otkel stories when I'm dead?* he thought. *What kind of stories will they be?* He noticed the woman leaving, crippled Jem—stuffed with rich foods—sleeping over her shoulder. He came to sudden decision.

"Wait!" he cried out to her. "Don't leave yet!" He snatched up his axe, stood, ran across the greathall to Thorolf's room, plunged in.

The three keys burned in his pouch, but he knew he could manage without them. With his axe, he attacked the log strongbox. Men came to the door and stared in amazement. Otkel was a powerful axeman, and he had the chest open in less time than anybody would have believed. The locks and iron bands still held; the end was gone. "Leif! Hermund! Come help!" The three of them lifted the strongbox, poured out a rich hoard of silver and gold and bronze. There were silver rings and brooches glinting, and the warm glow of a golden torc. On top of the pile was a wonderful brooch, gold and silver and copper animals glistening against an enameled background. Gemstones winked in the eyes of the animals. Other things were there as well, carnelian and glass beads, and carven figures made of walrus ivory.

"Tonight, none of Thorolf's friends leaves our hall without a gift!" He searched through the treasures, found a necklace of carnelian interspaced with silver pendants from the Skraeling kingdoms to the south and west. He motioned the woman forward, placed it about her neck. He bent again, picked out a small silver cloak-pin for Jem. He embraced the two of them. "Go now. Remember."

He turned to the others. "Leif, you were Thorolf's closest friend. You should have this golden torc. Hermund...."

By the time he was through, Otkel had even given a bronze cloak pin to the bailiff's man, Rhys.

The gifting had pretty well crowned the feast, and people quietly began to slip out until Otkel and the others were alone. Otkel raised his hands for silence. "Men, tomorrow will be busy. It's time to sleep. We'll rise a couple hours after the sun." He instructed a servant to wake them, and another to see to the horses they'd left back at the Sacred Grove.

The men were pulling out their bearskins and blankets, making up beds on the benches around the hall. Otkel headed toward his room, then thought of the sadly-diminished pile of silver lying on the floor in Thorolf's room. *Let's be sure it's still as big in the morning,* he thought. He went through the other door, threw off his clothes, and sank into heaped white bear furs. He slept.

In the hall, the light of the rising moon shone in the still-open windows. The dying fire cast a ruddy glow. Leif and Hermund, sleepless, were talking quietly. "Otkel has been a much better leader today than we could have expected," Hermund began.

"That's very true," Leif agreed. "He certainly gave Thorolf a funeral to be proud of!"

"*We all* gave Thorolf a funeral to be proud of," growled Starkad sleepily.

"Right. But Otkel was there at our head while we did it. And he gave us a very good bragarfull oath to swear." Hermund sank back on his furs, wriggled to a more comfortable position.

"It was a good oath, but there was one thing about it that puzzled me." Leif hesitated. There were inquiring grunts from Hermund and Starkad.

"Why did he call Odin's curse, and our vengeance, down upon the person that *dishonored* Thorolf, instead of the one that killed him?" Leif, too, lay down his head. There was silence. Soon all were asleep.

Chapter 8
Tuesday: More Troubles

Gervase and his men stood near the fairgrounds' tavern. The Eastern sky flamed red across the river. The morning mist was taken by the wind that had risen during the night. Leaf-rattle challenged the roar of the falls. Several morning fires were burning, smoke trailing close to the ground, but most of the camp was just beginning to wake. The grass was wet with dew.

One of the troopers wrapped his cloak a bit more tightly around himself. "There'll be a storm before we see tomorrow's sun. Red sky at morning...."

"There'll be a storm from the north, if we don't solve this killing before Ragnar and Otkel go to battle over it," Gervase noted. "And lightning from the castle. The baron and I watched Thorolf's pyre from the tower keep. He feels these fairs are our wealth, and he's going to have *somebody's* head if this one is spoiled. He'd prefer the killer's head, but one of ours will do."

The bailiff drew his troopers closer together. "After the pyre, Otkel and his men were feasting and drinking late. They won't be up for a while. We can concentrate on Ragnar. You, you, you – watch him, and Olaf, and that cook. Be careful around the cook, I'm told he never sleeps. The rest of us can talk with people, see what we can hear. Yesterday..." Four loud hoofbeats sounded on the bridge.

"Bailiff! Bailiff!" The rider's left boot was stained with blood from a cut on his leg. Judging by the way he sat his horse, it wasn't deep. "Highwaymen! Back where the road branches off to the lakes!" Suddenly everybody was running for the horses tethered to the tavern rail.

"Pestilence!" Gervase put his foot into the stirrup. "I would've worn mail if I'd been expecting a fight!" He swung his other leg over. The harness creaked. All about him, horses snorted in surprise. They'd just been tethered—they weren't expecting to be ridden again this soon.

His men were mounted. "Dirk! You stay here to investigate Ragnar! If we're lucky, these highwaymen will turn out to be Thorolf's killers. But let's not bet everything on it, hm?" Gervase swept his arm forward and spurred his horse. He and the troopers thundered across the bridge and out onto the road. The rider who'd brought the news trailed behind, his horse laboring.

Well, well, Dirk thought as he watched them disappear behind a screen of trees. *Now how did we go about investigating yesterday?* He scratched his stubble as his nose twitched. Tony was heating hard cider at the tavern, the wind carried the smell very clearly. And here came half-a-dozen traders, drawn by the commotion.

Time to grease a few tongues, and do some listening. Dirk rubbed his hands together. He sat at the largest table. "Cider, Tony!" he cried. "Lots of it, as hard as you have, and keep it coming. And a loaf of bread. Two loaves." He tossed the tavernkeeper a sixpence. That should last the morning.

He tore off a huge chunk of bread and dipped it in his mug of cider, chewed slowly, washed it down. Tony set down more mugs, steam writhing over the surface of the brown liquid for an instant before the wind snatched it away.

Dirk shoved a mug at the nearest merchant. "It's a cold morning, men. Warm yourselves."

He leaned back, lifted his mug expansively. "We may have this Thorolf thing sewed up tight as a miser's purse. The bailiff is after a pack of highwaymen this very moment."

A sour little man in eastern silk, skinny hands wrapped around the warm mug, disagreed. "Always highwaymen when merchants gather. Lord knows they do kill." His gaze swept them from beneath dark brows.

"When's last time highwayman's victim found with silver still on him?" He tossed a scrap of bread on the ground. A dog snapped it up, stood grinning for more. "Taking lazy way out, you think highwaymen did it."

He drank. "I don't mind. Thorolf's killer did us favor. Go after highwaymen with my blessing."

Dirk had been hoping for something a bit more useful in the way of disagreement. He shifted tactics. "You're right as can be." He set down his mug and held his right hand up, curled as if around a hilt. "We can do without those highwaymen, and we can probably do pretty well without Thorolf, too.

"Who else might we do without? Who else is unpopular?"

Dirk leaned back against the table-stump, pulled his hood down so his eyes were shaded against the rising sun. He drank, then rested quietly. Drops of cider sparkled in his stubble. The others drank and ate, and the wind carried away any slight sounds they made. The dog waited nearby, tongue lolling out. The canvas fly flapped overhead. They could hear the clopping of hooves and the creaking of wheels as Maude came driving up with the supply wagon.

"It wasn't Matilda," a Southerner dressed in wrinkled cottons said. "I watched her get drunk until well after sunset."

"And my wife helped put her to bed," the cloth-merchant from the tent by the paddock said. "She was settled in for a long night, and a hard awakening."

"Let's make sure that alibi holds." Nobody could see Dirk's eyes beneath the hood. "Suppose she was only faking. And suppose Thorolf was riding back after dark, with a torch. Matilda was a good enough archer to settle him, under those conditions. Then she'd just have to get rid of the torch, and everybody would think the murder happened at sundown when dozens of people were watching her at the tavern."

The clothman laughed. "You've missed your calling – you should tell tales in the market for coppers. You'd die rich. But I'm a light sleeper when my goods are in a tent, and I heard her snoring all night long. That funny little chirp? She was making it even before my wife had her bedded in. And I haven't heard about any torch-marks near Thorolf's body."

"Matilda's innocent," the Easterner said flatly. "Good thing. Need her horses. Don't trust Thorolf's lieutenant, though."

"Otkel?"

"That his name? Watched the two. Saw him when he thought nobody looking. Seems sort to want it all. Wouldn't trust him behind back."

Dirk pushed his hood back, ran his hand through his sandy hair. "Ragnar suggested much the same thing. Otkel's one of the slipperiest eelpouts I've ever known—but wasn't he with Thorolf's other men all that evening?"

"Maybe Thorolf riding at midnight with torch?"

"That's as silly with Otkel as it was with Matilda," the cloth-merchant sniffed. "Anyway, Otkel has the money to hire an assassin."

"I can't see Otkel trusting somebody else to keep his mouth shut." Dirk curled his lip. "Maybe we should see if any assassins have turned up dead?"

"Most merchants rich enough for assassin," the Easterner said. "You, me – Ragnar. Alibi useless, investigation dead. Go chase highwaymen."

"Ragnar wouldn't hire an assassin. Northmen would rather kill their enemies personally. That's a difference that would make *any* Northman reluctant to hire the job done. Besides, if Ragnar used an assassin, sure as bears eat berries he'd have an alibi—and he doesn't." Dirk leaned back.

Tony was refilling the mugs from a warming-pan of cider. He held the handle wrapped in his apron. "A tavernkeeper hears things, Dirk. You should include me in these little affairs of yours."

Tony reached for an empty mug, filled it. The merchants made room for him. He sat, sipped. "Otkel doesn't have an alibi either."

"There was a Finn here yesterday, talking with a Northman. Complaining, really." Tony drank again. "Finns are strange. Half of them are enchanters, and the other half *think* they're enchanters.

"He was saying a Northman had ruined the Skraeling burial-mound. Now sensible people wouldn't go near the place—haunted, like as not. Remember how careful the abbey drew its borders to keep the mound out? But Finns think those mounds are fine places for enchantments. Nobody but the Skraelings have ever invoked their gods there, and that was long years ago. 'Makes the spirits grateful for a bit of attention', they say.

"He was there an hour or so before sunset, day before yesterday. He wanted to do some enchantments for a successful Fair. Somebody got there ahead of him, and the Finn watched him put up a rune-staff on top of the mound and chant verse. Otkel was the one who did it. All the merchants here know what he looks like, so we can trust the identification.

"That mound is in the woods near where Thorolf's body was found."

There was a flat *whap!* and Gervase' horse screamed and stumbled. Gervase managed to kick his feet free of the stirrups, his body free of the falling horse. He hit on his shoulder, rolled, fetched up in a bush by the side of the trail with his feet over his head and a branch poking through the skirt of his tunic.

Crossbow, he thought as his mind caught up with him.

Most of his men had managed to rein their horses in, but one had tripped. Gervase' horse was screaming and thrashing wildly on the ground. The other was snorting and getting back to its feet. Its rider was cursing. He'd landed on a rock, cut a gash in his hip.

Gervase heard crashings and shouts, a clank of sword against metal, a *chunk!*, a shriek cut short by another *chunk!*

He untangled himself, pulled his tunic loose from the branch. His horse kicked, and died. The bailiff hugged the ground, in case there were more crossbow bolts where the last one came from.

"It's clear!" a trooper shouted from ahead. "They only left one rear-guard. I killed him!"

Somebody went to help the man who hit the rock. Gervase and the others went to the man who shouted. He stood, breathing hard; there was blood on his shortsword. A body lay nearby.

The dead ruffian wore a rusty iron cap, with a shiny crease on the left from a sword-blow. His right forearm had a deep wound, and his neck was cut halfway through. A heavy crossbow with a windlass was flung to one side, cocked but without a bolt. A quiver of bolts spilled over, and one lay beside the man's right hand. The corpse was unshaven, and his clothes were much the worse for wear.

"Damnation!" Gervase swore. "This man's equipped like a soldier. We're lucky a military crossbow takes so long to cock, but it means we're up against well-armed men. I hope we're dealing with deserters—I don't want to face somebody's raiding party."

Gervase saw something at the man's shoulder, and turned the corpse over with his foot. The smell of sudden death rose. The corpse had a long sword in a back scabbard.

"Men," the bailiff said, "we must be living properly. We weren't ready for a fight like this. Now here's a bastard sword for me. And Rhys, you're good with a crossbow. Take this one. I feel better, now that we can shoot back."

Gervase drew the dead man's sword and took a stance, feet apart and legs slightly bent. He moved the sword through a horizontal figure eight in front of him, swept the point through circles. His right hand held steady by the crossguard, while his left directed the large motions of the blade with quick economic motions of the pommel. "I *like* the balance!"

He made several swift feints, lopped a young aspen off at waist-height. "It'll do nicely." He took the highwayman's scabbard, buckled it at his shoulder.

Rhys had put a bolt in the crossbow. He fired. The heavy bolt shattered against a tree-trunk. "Shoots a bit to the left," the Welshman noted.

They went back to the trail. The others had bandaged the injured trooper's hip, but he was in no shape to fight. His horse seemed none the worse for its fall.

"Watch the body, Thomas," the bailiff told the trooper, "and try not to let anybody loot my saddle. We'll be back." There was a bit of quick horse-swapping, and they started off again down the path the highwaymen had taken.

The path led to a ford through a creek. One of the troopers was a tracker, and had taken the lead. He threw up his arm and pulled his horse to a stop. "They went into the water. They didn't come out."

Gervase looked hard at the trail. It was brown, beaten earth, with grass on either side. He couldn't tell the difference. Well, that was why they had a tracker.

"Do we go upstream, or down?" the bailiff asked. The tracker was off his horse, looking where the trail went into the water.

He pointed. "That hoofprint is smeared to the right. The horse turned upstream. It's the horseshoe with the mark I've been trailing." They splashed into the water.

The sun was up, and the wind blew through the trees. The day was getting hot, and the air was very damp by the flowing stream. Sunlight slanted through the trees on the east bank, casting moving shadows on the dappled water. Clouds were building up in the west. A deerfly bit Gervase on the back of the neck; he slapped viciously, listened to the departing buzz. They could barely hear the creek chuckling over rocks in a small rapids, with the noise of the wind rattling leaves.

Above the rapids the stream swelled into a pool, with marsh-grass in the shallows. Even Gervase could see the trail of bent and broken stalks where horses had waded in to shore. Half a dozen men were hurriedly breaking camp in a clearing. They were packing things into saddle-bags, and loading up the one pack-horse. Their horses were not very good.

One of the men looked up, pointed at them.

"*Take them*!" Gervase roared. He spurred his horse through the pool of grass, followed by the troopers.

The highwaymen might have once been soldiers, but they weren't disciplined. Instead of acting together, two of them snatched up weapons and prepared to make a defense. The others leaped on their horses and rode into the woods. One grabbed the halter of the pack-horse, and led it behind him.

Gervase pulled the sword as he rode, holding it one-handed. He charged the nearest brigand, took a vicious swipe at him, but his horse shied away. It had already had one tumble, seen another horse die. It was not about to risk its life for a strange rider.

The bailiff looked at the two highwaymen. Nothing but shortsword and buckler, the both of them. Rhys hit one highwayman's buckler with a crossbow bolt, and he broke and ran. Three troopers circled him on horses, harried him back into the clearing.

I can take this churl, Gervase thought. He found himself on the ground running toward the remaining brigand, with no clear memory of getting off his horse.

The highwayman cut downwards at him. Gervase slapped the blade aside with his sword, held the momentum, brought his bastard sword up, over, down at his opponent's head. The man punched out with his buckler, blocked the blow, snapped his sword out at the Bailiff's midriff.

Gervase jumped back, spun his sword downwards to take the brigand's sword-arm. But the arm wasn't there; it was circling down, behind, up, coming at Gervase with a blow from above.

The bailiff deflected it, blade still down, and stepped forward to land a heavy blow with his pommel onto the brigand's helmet.

The man staggered, then turned tail and ran. Gervase heard hoofbeats pounding up behind him, prayed briefly they were his troopers. He threw himself forward, swung his sword backhanded at the fleeing robber, just nicked the back of his leg with the tip of his sword.

The man stumbled, fell, tried to get up. He couldn't. His foot was at a peculiar angle. He got to his knees, brought up his buckler, then crouched behind it, glaring like a snapping-turtle, sword at the ready. There was a trickle of blood coming from his ankle.

Gervase looked around the clearing. Three troopers had ridden up to join him. The other highwayman was dead. The camp was silent, except for the snorting of horses and the curses of the injured brigand. A wisp of smoke rose from a poorly-quenched campfire.

"We'll clear all this up later." Gervase ran for his horse. "Let's get the ones that rode for it."

"What about him?" one of his men asked, jerking a thumb at the brigand with the sword.

"Leave him. He's still dangerous, but he's hamstrung. How's he going to escape, hm? And if he does, he'll never be a highwayman again. He'll be a beggar." Gervase swung into the saddle.

"Can't I shoot him?" asked Rhys, cradling the crossbow.

"Don't waste the bolt. Keep that crossbow cocked and ready."

"I'll not quarrel," Rhys agreed. They followed the tracker into the woods.

Behind them the injured robber cursed, set down his weapons, pulled himself up by the trunk of a birch. He tried to take a cautious step, and fell. Gervase could hear him begin to weep. *Maybe it would have been kinder to kill him,* the bailiff thought to himself. *But it's not our job to make life and death easier for highwaymen.*

The trail was clear. The bandits were panicked, had no time or care for stealth. Soon Gervase and his troopers were close on the heels of the bandits, whose horses were a sorry lot. The one leading the pack-horse let go of its reins, and it fell behind.

One of the bandits had a horseman's bow. An arrow whipped past Gervase' ear, shattered against a tree-trunk. Rhys' crossbow shot with a whap! The bandit cried out and clutched his shoulder, barely staying in his saddle. "Good man!" Gervase yelled to Rhys.

"I was aiming for his chest," Rhys shouted back. "This crossbow *definitely* shoots to the left."

There were three highwaymen left—four with the one Rhys shot. Gervase and four troopers were chasing them. The robber on the best horse screamed "Scatter!" and pulled off to the left. One went ahead, one to the right. The wounded rider let his horse slow to a stop.

"I'll take the one I shot!" Rhys shouted as he slowed.

Gervase motioned to the trooper closest to him, and took after the robber with the good horse. "That looks like their chief!"

The other two troopers split up to follow the remaining two bandits.

The bandit chief had left the trail. Tree-branches whipped at their faces and bodies. Ferns and bushes hid the ground. A branch snagged Gervase's tunic, almost pulled him off his horse. His trooper surged ahead, swung his shortsword at the bandit. The bandit ducked, swung back. Their swords clashed with a dull sound. The trooper's horse wheeled so he could wield his sword more comfortably.

That bandit's a good fighter, Gervase thought as he spurred forward. *But it sounds like his sword is made from soft iron.* He closed in with his longer sword, feinted a stroke at the bandit, but focussed his aim on the bandit's sword. He hit. The shorter sword bent nearly at a right angle, was torn from the bandit's hand. Before the man could recover, the trooper reached out, grabbed the bandit's arm, and pulled him from his horse. He hit the ground, and Gervase landed on him heavily. Air whooshed out of the bandit, and by the time he'd recovered his breath, his hands were tied behind him.

"Catch his horse and get the sword," Gervase said. "Then we'll go back to where we split up. I think the baron has a few men that might want to ask these fellows questions." And they began finishing up the chase and capture.

Chapter 9
Tuesday: The Rune-Staff

Ragnar Forkbeard was sipping his morning broth—Gunnar had made it from yesterday's leftover stew—when he heard a commotion by the tavern. It was louder, even, than the wind and the falls. He moved to the front of his booth in time to watch the bailiff and his troopers riding out in a great hurry. Another rider was straggling behind. Ragnar stood there, bowl in one hand and bread in the other. "Ari! Get over to the tavern and find out what's happening!" Ari hustled off.

"That strange rider was wounded. He had blood on his boot and breeches," Atli noted.

Ari came back. "Highwaymen wounded a rider on the lake road, near where Thorolf was killed, but he managed to escape them. The bailiff and his men rode to catch the bandits. He left his deputy here to investigate you. He's buying cider for the merchants to get them to talk."

"Is he, then? You and Atli visit the tavern and see what people are talking about. Watch over each other like the brothers you are. And—" Ragnar tossed a small pouch to Ari, "—use this silver to buy drinks for merchants yourself."

"Ah," Ari said. "Atli and I are rising in the world of merchants. We need to make friends."

"With that much silver, I wouldn't be surprised if Tony over at the tavern became your friend." Olaf Far-traveler grinned. He'd wandered over to see what the fuss was.

"Today will probably be interesting," Ragnar told Olaf. "Those highwaymen might keep the bailiff busy all day long. Like as not, Otkel and his crew will be here well before the bailiff returns."

"You think they're Otkel's men now?"

"Atli was at the sacred grove much of yesterday. It looked that way to him."

Olaf looked at the sky, smelled the wind, listened to the leaves rattling. "And we're going to have a storm, too. We'd better all stay around the booths and the boats, and batten down for weather before it comes."

"You have the right of it. Remember, we may get foul weather from Otkel and the bailiff, as well as the sky. I hope they decide those highwaymen are the ones who killed Thorolf, but we can't count on that."

"Thorolf is even more trouble dead than he was alive," Olaf said sourly.

"It's often that way. Snorri Crow gave Thorolf a lot of trouble after *he* was dead."

"Well, Thorolf shouldn't have killed him, then."

"Sometimes a killing is worth the trouble. If I had a good shot at Thorolf, I might have been tempted to kill him myself, even here in the lands of the English. I could go trading to Miklagard with you, if the English made a fuss."

"We may end up doing that anyway, unless somebody sorts out this Thorolf mess. But Lakesend has the Miklagard trade in bulk iron firmly in their grasp." Olaf shrugged his shoulders. "You might do better with finished goods in the Algonquin towns along the way. They're an eager market for kettles, knives, hatchets, and arrowheads. You can get nice furs from them, also beadwork and tobacco."

"Oh, right, tobacco. As if I don't get enough smoke when I'm in the smithy!"

"I agree, but some people will pay a lot for the stuff."

"Agh, the trolls take tobacco! And Otkel too, while they're at it." Ragnar spat on the ground. "It's time to start getting ready for today's trading. We'll plan next year's ventures some other time." He dipped his bread in broth gone cold, tore a chunk off with his teeth. Then he went to the cookfire and had Gunnar warm the bowl with some fresh broth. He ate the bread, drank the broth, and cautioned Gunnar to make lots of bread so they would have something to eat during the storm. Then he went into his booth to change clothes.

The morning was a strange mix of caution and carelessness. Merchants didn't have as much on display, because they could see the weather was turning toward a storm. This was doubly true for cloth-merchants and others with goods that could be taken by the wind.

At the tavern, Tony and his wife Maude had finished transferring the food and drink from their supply wagon to Tony's enclosed wagon. "Get back to Milltown and take care of the inn," Tony told her. "With the storm that looks to be coming, we'll need somebody responsible there. Then after the storm, as soon as the ferry looks safe, bring more supplies. Business is always brisk after a storm—everybody's too busy fixing up their camp to cook." He gave her a hug, and she drove the wagon back the way they had come.

Everybody was seeing to their shelter. The merchants with stone booths had it easy—all they had to do was make sure their canvas roofs were fastened well and tightly. People with tents and pavilions were setting out extra lines and stakes, adjusting their groundcloths, and making sure there were no potential leaks. Olaf and Ragnar sent their best ship-handlers to make sure their boats were pulled higher on the riverbank, covered with canvas, and staked down.

At the same time, merchants were trading feverishly. They wanted to sell as much as they could. They were out from under the shadow of Thorolf, but his servants had been by the previous afternoon warning them to hold by their deals. Nobody knew what Otkel would be like, but they suspected he would *not* be pleasant. If they sold their goods rapidly, they could leave for home before Otkel got to them.

Ari and Atli had no sooner reached the tavern than they heard Tony say that Otkel had been seen putting up a rune-staff on the Skraeling mound. Atli brought Ragnar the news.

Ragnar's eyes opened wide. "A rune-staff? Chanting? And this was late in the afternoon of the day Thorolf was killed? If that staff was a scorn-pole, we need to find out who it was cursing!" He stood. "You handle the trading for a while, Knute. I'm going to talk with the deputy. Atli, get back to handing out drinks and listening." Ragnar and Atli walked off vigorously.

Dirk Cachepol was being an open-handed host at the largest of the tables. There was bread at the table, and a kettle of warm cider. There were a few prosperous merchants with him, but mostly carters, drovers, porters, and the like—the sort that love their gossip and drift toward free drinks and food. Ragnar picked up a cup, filled it from the kettle, and went over to the deputy. "Dirk, might I have a word with you in private?"

Dirk cocked his head at him, and grunted assent. He stood. The two walked a ways toward the river. When they were out of earshot of the rest, Dirk asked, "Going to tell me to back off?"

"Not at all. A merchant investigates his situation. You keep order, and that takes investigation too."

Dirk nodded.

"I just want to make sure you do a thorough and proper investigation. Killings are serious matters, and I want serious consideration of *all* the suspects. If those rumors of Otkel and the rune-staff are true, you should get that staff to the priests of the sacred grove. They can tell a lot from the runes carved into it. Rune-staves are powerful; Egil Skallagrimsson set one up against King Eirik Bloodaxe of Norway, and it wasn't that long until Hakon the Good chased Eirik out and took over as king instead."

Dirk smiled a crooked smile in consideration. "I've sent out word I'd like to talk with the Finn who spoke of it. But you make a good argument. You and I should go there together to get the staff."

Ragnar nodded. "There are highwaymen in that direction. We should take a few strong, honest men with us. It'll be safer, and any dispute won't be just your word against mine."

They were still carrying their cups of cider. They raised them to each other, and drank. "I have to make arrangements at my booth," Ragnar said. "A lot of the merchants came with guards. See if you can borrow a few. I'll meet you at the tavern."

Soon Ragnar was back, riding a horse. He'd put on a steel cap and mail shirt, his bow was on his saddle, a longsword was strapped to his belt, and he carried a small shield in his left hand. He had an extra mail shirt for Dirk. "Best to be ready."

Dirk shrugged into the mail. "Thanks."

Soon they were headed down the road to Northlanding, accompanied by four guards. They'd been loaned by a southern spice merchant looking to curry some favor with the baronial officials. Dirk snickered to himself over *that*. Dirk guided them—he was local, he knew the way. Somewhere after the lake road, but before the abbey road, he reined his horse to a stop and pointed away from the river into the brush and trees alongside the road. "The Skraeling mound is that way. We can ride there."

The horses were reluctant, but the men urged them into the woods. Once they were past the undergrowth at the edge of the trees, the ground cover thinned out. The sun was high enough to give good light, but low enough to give them direction. They rode in single file behind Dirk. Mostly, they followed his hand-signals, because the noise of the wind in the trees was enough to drown their voices.

The land began to rise, and it was softer. There weren't as many rocks, and the trees were stunted by the sandy soil. As they neared the top of the mound, trees gave way to grass. Near the center of the clearing was a fresh staff planted into the ground. As they came closer, they could see carved and painted runes. The skull of a horse lay on the ground, facing back the way they had come.

The mound was high enough that they could see over the trees in several directions. Wind blew and branches swayed, and it seemed to Ragnar that they were surrounded by green and wave-tossed waters. "This doesn't look auspicious. We should get to the sacred grove before the storm breaks." He dismounted and put the skull in a saddlebag, being careful not to touch it with his flesh, and plucked up the staff. He mounted and turned his horse back toward the road. "Let's travel."

Ragnar and Dirk left their horses and the guards in the stable of the sacred grove. Gunnvald the high priest, a gaunt old fellow with a silver beard and a gray robe, was at the door to the temple longhouse. Ragnar showed him the staff, and handed him the saddlebag with the horse's skull. The priest opened the saddlebag, looked the skull over. "This doesn't seem anything special." He put it on a table near the entrance.

He took the staff outdoors for the best light to examine the runes, his face growing more sour as time went on. "Whoever carved this was no rune-master. It looks like it was intended to draw wealth to the carver. But it's careless enough that it could have cursed half the merchants in town. Or maybe the other way around. Where was the horse's skull?"

"It was on the ground at the base of the staff, facing toward the river."

Dirk spent some time thinking. "Facing a bit downstream, and it was tilted to one side."

"The skull is supposed to be at the top of the staff. It must have blown off in this wind. Pity. If it'd stayed in place, we would have known where the spell was aimed." The priest frowned. "We should burn that staff. Its runes are too ill-formed and dangerous to keep around."

"Could you wait on that?" Dirk asked. "That staff might mean something about the death of Thorolf Pike. We may need its testimony, and yours."

The priest turned to walk into the longhouse. "Come with me then. Bear witness." He brought the staff to the statue of Odin, taller than a man, covered in gold-leaf, seated on a high-seat and holding his spear Gungnir. Carved ravens, stained black as night, were on the shoulders of the god. They had glistening obsidian eyes. There was a spear-holder before the statue.

The priest knelt before the statue, the rune-staff horizontal in his outstretched hands. "Odin All-Father, guard us as we search for truth." He stood, placed the staff in the spear-holder, and prostrated himself before the statue. *"You know a rune, a sixth mighty rune. It saves us if a man cuts runes on a sapling's roots with intent to harm. It turns the spell. The hater is harmed, not we."* He stood and bowed his head. "The words of the High One."

He looked at them. "We will hold the staff for one cycle of the moon, starting with Thorolf's pyre last night. Then it, too, shall burn."

"That should be quite enough," Dirk replied.

"Many thanks for your aid and wisdom," Ragnar turned to go. He hesitated, drew forth the dagger on his belt, gave it to the priest. "Hang this on the sacrifice oak. It is of my making."

The priest looked it over. "Your runes are well-formed."

"Thank you," Ragnar replied. Then he and Dirk went out into the light and the wind. It was coming up on noon. The sun was shining, but dark clouds scudded by to the south, edging closer.

Dirk looked back at the temple. "I've not been here before. The statues are magnificent, at least as handsome as those in the cathedral."

"The statues in the cathedral are mostly just saints. Our temple has *gods*. Of course we'd have them carved by our finest artisans. The gods might get angry if we didn't do our best."

They went to the stables, and soon were riding back toward the fairgrounds. The guards followed along. They saw no evidence of highwaymen, nor of the bailiff and troopers. Dirk was anxious about that, but he had his instructions. He was to investigate Ragnar, and this certainly counted as close observation.

Ragnar saw Dirk looking at the ground near the lake road, along the side-road and into the bushes. There was a spatter of blood on the road. "This is where the robbers were reported?"

"Yes, curse them. We're having enough trouble over Thorolf, without bandits too. I hope our men are okay." The borrowed guards were close enough to hear this, and paid closer attention to their surroundings for some while.

When they reached the fairgrounds, Otkel and his men were by Matilda's paddock. Starkad was threatening Matilda. Benedict stood between the two, looking small but determined.

"I've been told you were very rude to Thorolf, his last day alive," Otkel said in a deadly voice. Starkad growled, and worked his shoulders. Judging by their faces, Otkel's other men had mixed reactions. Some agreed with Starkad, while others—Leif chief among them—knew that Thorolf had been fond of Matilda and wouldn't want her harmed.

Benedict stayed between Starkad and Matilda, but spoke to Otkel. "God's wounds, Otkel, don't you realize? Thorolf was always the voice of moderation in your dealings. He wouldn't approve, no he wouldn't! Whatever else, he *liked* Matilda!"

Ragnar and Dirk were hurrying toward the paddock, but Olaf Far-traveler beat them to it. He leaped the fence, grappled Starkad by the waist, and threw him into the water-trough. Otkel snatched his axe from where it rested on his shoulder, while Starkad spluttered in the water.

"Haw!" Olaf bellowed. "If that water's for horses, it should do for an ass!" Then he raised his open, empty hands, one toward Otkel and one toward Starkad. "They hang killers in Northlanding. It's a strange law, but I'm beginning to appreciate it. It'd be a shameful death for anyone who kills me, and I'd have my revenge. So—" he motioned a come-on to Starkad and Otkel "—want to wrestle?" He made the sign of Thor's Hammer, as his teeth glinted in a fierce smile.

But Otkel and Starkad didn't want to wrestle. Ragnar, Dirk, and the guards had arrived, well-armed and armored. More of Olaf's and Ragnar's men were coming up each moment. A lot of merchants had seen what was happening, and sent their guards. Otkel had a dozen men, but suddenly that didn't seem like many. He hung his axe back on his shoulder.

After that, Otkel and his men went about trying to make merchants hold by their deals with Thorolf. But Dirk, guards, and other armed men followed Otkel around, and the merchants had seen him back down at Matilda's. They were not about to accept deals that had seemed reasonable only when Thorolf was there to propose them.

Otkel first went to the tent of a merchant who had crossed the Cold Sea to Lakesend with a shipload of copper ingots. He was a stranger to this trade fair, and Otkel thought he might be easily intimidated. "You promised us copper at the price of iron. We're here to get it."

"I promised Thorolf copper at that price," the man replied. "Everybody told me Thorolf was a powerful man. His favor was worth cultivating, and his disfavor best avoided. Bring Thorolf with you, and you can have the copper."

"Unpleasant things might happen," Otkel said.

"In a few days the fair will be over, and I'll be on the road to Lakesend. Soon after that, I'll be far away at sea. If something unpleasant wants to happen to me here, it had better hurry." He looked at the guards following Otkel and his men.

Otkel decided it would be wiser to seek a local merchant, one he had better relations with. He went over to the dyer's booth. The dyer was out in front with samples of his work. He had acquired much undyed linen and wool, stored in his booth, and he had dyestuffs to sell and trade. "Good day, Samuel."

"And a good day to you, Otkel, such as you can have in these terrible times. I was saddened to hear of Thorolf's death."

"It was a shock to all of us. But we're trying to uphold the deals he made."

"A man's word is important," Samuel agreed. "And I have the cochineal I promised you. Have you gotten the alum from those traders to the west, for the exchange?"

"I haven't talked to them yet today. They didn't deliver yesterday like they promised they would."

"Undoubtedly they didn't want to intrude upon you in your grief. I haven't forgotten the help you and Thorolf gave me setting up in the southwest trade, and as soon as you have the alum I'll give you your cochineal at a very favorable rate."

Otkel left then, and his men followed. "That wasn't bad, nor was it good. But I think we can make this one work. We have alum in our warehouse. If those other traders don't come through, we can still make a profit on the cochineal."

"People aren't cooperating," Leif noted the obvious. Starkad growled in agreement, his face dark with annoyance.

Otkel looked decisive. "We'll talk with locals. They can't go away across the sea, so they'll have to be more agreeable." Everybody nodded at that, and Otkel strode off toward James Smith's booth.

James was busy at his small forge, repairing and sharpening a camp hatchet. "I can't talk now, Otkel. People need things fixed. There's a storm headed this way, and they have to be ready." He swept his hammer-arm up toward the clouds, which were starting to overcome the sun.

Otkel couldn't deny that. "Yesterday was bad, and today isn't any better," he told his men. "Nothing will be improved by our getting rained on. Let's go home. I want to take an inventory. We might be able to make some profit yet, if we use goods we already have."

Chapter 10
Tuesday: The Raven Circles

On their way back to Northlanding, Otkel and his men saw the bailiff and his troopers with a group of prisoners. Otkel rode ahead and hailed the bailiff. "What's this?"

Gervase smiled grimly. "We caught some highwaymen that were making trouble earlier today. Most of them are even in shape to talk."

Otkel looked them over. They were a scruffy lot. "That's quite a few highwaymen, but only one of your troopers seems wounded. Two of the bandits appear dead. You must have fought very fiercely."

"They ran," Gervase said, "and they didn't all run at the same speed. We took them a few at a time. That's the way to do it, hm?"

"Any way you take highwaymen is good, but the easy ways are best. Can we help you bring them in?"

"Why, *thank* you, Otkel! We could use help with their camp goods, and you seem to have a few extra pack horses. With your help, we might all get home before the rain hits."

Otkel winced inside at the mention of 'extra pack horses.' Those horses were supposed to be carrying trade goods. But he motioned his men forward. "Load our horses," he told them. Then he turned back to the bailiff. "Did these robbers have anything to do with Thorolf's death?"

Gervase shrugged. "I doubt it. None of them had the right kind of bow to shoot the arrow that killed Thorolf. The baron's men will question them, and that will be one of the questions."

"Another reason to get them to the baron in a hurry. Besides, that one with the wounded shoulder doesn't look like he'll keep very well."

The robbers traveled slowly—they were bruised and hurt, and did *not* want to go to the castle—but they had no choice. The procession beat the rain, arriving just as the clouds were overcoming the sun. They all went in the gate, across the courtyard, and into the keep. Gervase called for the physician, and some men-at-arms.

Otkel and his men, helped by a man-at-arms, tossed the dead highwaymen in one cell, and all their goods in another. Then the armsman locked the cells. The physician had gone right to the injured trooper. He had his apprentice working on the bandits. The bandits needed their wounds bound up, though the one Rhys had shot was in poor shape. "I don't think he'll make it," the apprentice said. The bandit Gervase had hamstrung would live, but forever be a cripple.

When the physician looked at the troopers, he found most had a bad rash as well as relatively minor wounds. "Get that unguent from my office," he told a man-at-arms. "It's in a stoneware pot bearing the abbey's coat of arms."

Gervase had some wounds he hadn't even noticed, probably from the ground and the bushes. But at least he didn't have a rash.

While all this was going on, Otkel took Starkad aside. "I'd bet you're angry at Olaf Far-traveler," he said. Starkad scowled. His clothes were still damp from the soaking Olaf had given him, and the memory fresh. "Would you like to help give him and Ragnar Forkbeard some trouble?" Starkad bared his teeth in a fierce smile.

"When we killed Snorri Crow, Thorolf took his cloak-brooch as a trophy. It was one of the handsomest he'd ever seen. I saw it last night, in the trove we were gifting from. I want you to get that brooch, quietly so nobody else notices. Then take it to the fairgrounds. Leave it somewhere around Olaf's booth, like it was dropped by accident. With the storm we have coming, everybody will be under cover and won't see you. I'll talk with the bailiff, and do the rest."

Then Otkel gathered his men. "You should all go back to the warehouse and work on inventory for tomorrow's trading. I'll stay here and talk with the bailiff. Maybe I can help him find Thorolf's killer."

The Northmen left, taking their horses with them. Outside, the wind had died down, but the air smelled of water. Otkel leaned against the wall near the door, watching and listening. The armsmen and the troopers were busy getting the robbers into a cell. The man Gervase called the leader was put in a separate cell, and the baron's questioners carried off the man with the shoulder wound. *That's smart,* Otkel thought. *You can never tell what you'll hear from a dying man, but it'll likely be more useful than asking questions after he's dead.*

Finally the bailiff dismissed his troopers to their quarters, and came over to Otkel. "Did you have something you wanted to say?"

Otkel had been considering that very matter. "I've been thinking back on Thorolf's body."

The door rattled as the wind picked up again, and they could hear the rush of rain against the oiled-parchment windows. "You wouldn't want to go out in that weather, hm? Come with me. It's been a hard day, and we could use some wine while we talk." Gervase motioned to a servant. "Light the candles, and bring warm spiced wine to my quarters."

The servant trotted up the spiral staircase. Gervase and Otkel followed in a more leisurely fashion. By the time they'd reached the second landing, candlelight was spilling out through a doorway as the servant hustled back through the door. Gervase entered and went to the window, drew back the parchment to look out. "Oh, that's nasty," he murmured. Otkel looked, and agreed. It was still mid-afternoon, but dark as dusk. He couldn't see far through the downpour, but occasional flashes of lightning lit up trees tossing wildly in the wind. Pools of rainwater were gathering everywhere. The air was filled with thunder, and the roar of the wind.

The bailiff took a seat, motioned Otkel to another. Otkel looked around as he crossed the room. The outer walls were harsh stone, but candlelight shone on tapestries of hunting and hawking to brighten them. A small table held two candles, what looked like an account book, a small stack of cheap parchment, an inkwell, a writing frame, and a quill. On top of the parchment was a wax tablet and stylus for temporary notes. Against the far wall a framework held a mail shirt and helmet, with a steel breastplate over all. There was a comfortable-looking bed against the inside wall.

Gervase swept his arm to indicate the room. "Rank has its small privileges, hm? I hear you live well also." The servant returned with wine, and poured a cup for each of them. Then he left, quietly closing the door.

They sat and sipped, taking in the warmth of the wine. There was a comfortable silence.

"Thorolf's body?" the bailiff eventually murmured.

Otkel twitched, came back from his ruminations. "I was upset when I noticed his pouch of silver was gone. Sometimes you learn from what is *not* said, what is *not* there. Missing silver would speak of thieves." Otkel trailed off.

Gervase remembered the way Otkel had looked at him when he'd said he'd taken the pouch for evidence. Wisely, he held his tongue.

"When we were preparing Thorolf's body for the pyre, I noticed something else was gone: a brooch Thorolf was very fond of wearing, silver and copper and gold. And it doesn't seem to be around the warehouse, either."

Gervase raised an eyebrow. "Mm?"

"A missing brooch could speak of thieves. But this one speaks of Surtsheim, and the men of Snorri Crow. Thorolf took the brooch from him as a trophy. If one of Snorri's faction saw Thorolf wearing it, they might feel the need to reclaim it for Snorri's family."

"I think I follow you. That *does* sound like Northmen. And here we have thirty men of Surtsheim at the fair?"

"That's just so. Ragnar Forkbeard was one of Snorri's strongest supporters, and he brought about ten men. Olaf Far-traveler came to Surtsheim after Snorri died, but some of his men were of Snorri's faction. And ten or so men are travelling with them for the adventure and to do some trading of their own. I don't know them well, but they're from Surtsheim also."

"Ragnar told me none of his men, or Olaf's, had announced the killing of Thorolf."

"Ragnar is good at telling part-truths. But that still leaves Ragnar and Olaf, and the ten that are neither's men."

"I was wondering about that myself, but I hadn't known ten were neither man's men."

"Northmen are an independent lot. Most of those ten are young enough that they don't remember Snorri Crow well. And Olaf didn't come to Surtsheim until after we'd been outlawed. Ragnar Forkbeard is still the most likely killer."

"You've seemed very sure of that, even from the beginning."

"Bailiff, Thorolf's death was nowhere *near* the beginning of this. There's been bad blood between Thorolf and Ragnar for ten years and more."

"Hm."

Both men took sips of their wine, and breathed deeply of its scent. They listened to the storm in silence, took another sip. The candles flickered in the drafts that forced their way through the windows, past the parchment that kept out the rain. They were glad to be indoors.

After a while, Gervase spoke. "Let's assume Ragnar has the brooch. Let's assume it's proof he was involved in Thorolf's killing. How on earth would I find it?"

Otkel thought for a while. "Ragnar follows the laws and customs of Surtsheim district well. He's not as particular about other peoples' laws and customs. He wouldn't mind killing somebody despite *your* laws, so long as it were legal in Surtsheim. He'd be perfectly happy taking the King's Deer. If he thought he could underpay his tariff on this fair, he'd be doubly happy."

"Ragnar's cook made venison stew for the noon meal, yesterday," Gervase noted. "One of my men had a taste of it."

"Well then, send the gamekeepers out to see if they can find any evidence it was made from a local deer. And while they're poking around, who knows what else they might find?"

"You have a subtle mind, Otkel."

"Thank you."

At the tavern, Dirk joined tables with Atli and Ari. All three wanted to know what people were saying. Sitting together saved energy and money. Besides, they'd had enough hard cider themselves to feel companionable.

Soon enough, the wind was gusting even more strongly. Tony was cleaning up the area and storing everything. He was alone—his wife Maude was back in Milltown with their daughter, taking care of their inn. He had secured his wagon with stout pegs and strong ropes. "Help me get the canvas fly down." Ari and Atli took the ropes in hand to keep it from escaping, while Dirk undid the knots. They got it folded and into the wagon just as the first raindrops started splattering the ground. Tony climbed in, and pulled the doors shut behind him.

Dirk saw the real rain approaching. "I have to get this mail shirt off before it rusts and stains my clothes!" The three made a dash for Ragnar's booth. They were the last ones there, and as soon as they got in, the heavens opened. They slammed the door, and barred it. Rain rattled on the canvas roof. There was a tremendous clap of thunder.

"Whew!" Dirk said. "Help me out of this?" He bent over and held out his arms, and Atli pulled the mail shirt over his head.

Dirk turned his head toward Ragnar. "Thanks for the loan. Turned out I didn't need it, but I felt safer."

Ragnar took the shirt, and draped it over a wooden bar. "Self-interest, Dirk. If I'd left with a live deputy, and returned with a dead one, I'd never hear the end of it."

There was a strong burst of wind. A small branch blew from a tree and landed on the roof. They could see its faint shadow through the canvas. Another gust took it away. The roof tried to flap, but it was tied down too securely. A cold draft forced its way into the booth.

"Stay with us until the storm is over." Ragnar sat on his chair, and motioned Dirk to the stool. There were perhaps a dozen men in the booth, sitting on benches, rolls of bedding, and their traveling chests. Some were lying down already, preparing for a nap. There was a shadowy pile of moose antler toward the rear, and small chests of who-knows-what. A handsome bed with ornamented dragon posts stood against one wall, with bear furs on top.

Dirk looked the men over. None of them seemed eager to kill him. He relaxed.

Gunnar spoke up. "I started some ale as soon as we got here. Who wants to help strain it?" Knute, and several other men, jumped to their feet. Gunnar put a cloth over his brew-keg, while the men picked up the barrel. They carefully poured the ale through the cloth, which filled with barley mash as the ale itself went through to the keg.

Gunnar picked up the cloth, and squeezed the remaining liquid into the keg. "Breakfast porridge," he said with a smile as he lifted the bundle and put it into another kettle. "*If* we can light a cook-fire by then. Now, wait for the ale to settle."

The men had hustled much of the day, preparing for the storm, and they wanted to relax. They didn't wait long. Soon the cups and horns and bowls came out, and everybody began to drink. Gunnar broke out some bread and a chest of jerky, carried them around. "At least give the ale some food for company."

Ragnar went over, got a large bowl of ale, and brought it to Dirk himself. Then he went back and got himself a full horn. They leaned back, and drank. "Ah," Ragnar sighed. "It's young compared to Tony's ale. But Gunnar makes a good brew."

Several of the men broke into song, loud enough to be heard even over the wind and rain. Dirk got some bread and jerky, began to chew. The bread was soft, the jerky hard. He liked the contrast.

Ragnar sipped his ale as he looked the men over. They were dry, well-fed, quite jolly, and surrounded by a dangerous storm. It could be a good time for tales, but the noise of the wind probably ruled that out.

There was a loud crunch as something, blown by the wind, bounced off their walls. The light through the canvas roof was growing dim. Leaves rattled past in bunches, torn from the trees.

"Thor defend us," Ragnar said quietly. "I'm glad we're not at sea in this weather." Lightning and thunder answered.

"How often *have* you been at sea in weather like this?" Dirk asked, equally quietly.

"Often enough to satisfy me, but nowhere as often as Olaf. He trades to the east, and sails the big seas to get there. I just go to sea when I need copper, or fish. Most of the men in this booth have only been on the Little Sea. They don't know what it's like on the big seas."

The men were lying back, talking and singing. The air was getting chill with the storm, and they were starting to haul out their wool blankets.

"They don't seem worried," Dirk noted.

"They've been making things all winter. Then we had to load the boats, and move them down the river. Once we were here, we worked to set up for trade. They've been busy. Now, of a sudden, nobody—not even themselves—expects them to do anything. Of course they want to lean back."

Ragnar took another drink from his horn. "Young ale helps make us carefree, but we still have our wits about us. It's safe to relax, even in this weather. Of course, some of the men are young too. They haven't seen the things that can happen to a boat, or a merchant."

There was silence in the rear, as much as could be found in this storm, then Knute began to chant, in a carrying voice.

When comes winter   we will want to
Stay quite warm around the stead.
Hunting finds food   fire heats it,
Ale is good, and so is bed.

But we cannot   work at nothing
So we craft around the home
Stropping iron,   smithing silver,
Carving wood and shaping bone.

Polish bright stones   spin some linen,
Gifts for friends and family.
On the Solstice   flames the Yule-log
Celebrate around the tree.

Weather warming,   winter weakens
Makers start to seek to sell.
Crafting baubles,   spear-blades sharpen,
Trapping furs and tanning well.

Caching cargo   moving metal,
Stocking ships with goods and freight.
Riding rapids   rowing ripples
Drifting down Spring's water-spate.

Band of brothers   broach to landfall
On to Fair we gladly roam,
Show our goods forth   look at their goods,
Trade for goods we lack at home.

> Row up-river   breasting current
> Home to tell our travel-tale.
> Showing silver,   glass and grape-wine,
> And our comrades, safe and hale.

Ragnar smiled. "That was nicely done. Knute's voice is well on the way to being fit for a captain. If we can hear him over this storm, his crew can hear him at sea. And he translated the poem into English well." The others seemed to agree. They were clapping Knute's shoulder, grinning, raising their fists and shouting joyously. "Now all we have to do is get back safe and hale."

Gunnar came over to them. "The raven of death circles above us. We must be wary if we wish to return home safely. Pray to Thor to preserve us."

Ragnar looked into Gunnar's eyes. "This is one of your visions, isn't it?"

Gunnar nodded. "I only saw the raven. Nothing is certain." He went back among the other men, lay down, and wrapped himself in his blanket. He was silent and motionless, but Ragnar and Dirk could see his open eyes gleaming in the dimness.

Outside, wrapped in a dark cloak, Starkad dropped the brooch and nudged it under one of the sitting-logs near the cookfire circle. Then, buffeted by the wind, water streaming from him, he began the long walk back toward Northlanding.

Chapter 11
Wednesday: More Ravens

After an uneasy night, Benedict had finally sunk into a deeper slumber. Now daylight was starting to shine through small greased-rawhide windows. He began to stir.

He no longer heard the howl of the wind, nor the rush of rain. The storm was over.

He wasn't at home, safe in his own bed. His eyes opened, to the interior of a small shed. He was sleeping on a horse-blanket over hay. He'd gathered extra hay under it for a pillow, used his small cloak as best he could for cover, and wrapped any loose sections of the blanket around him for warmth. Where was he?

Then he noticed an exhalation, followed by a small chirp. *Ah, that was it,* he thought. *We were helping Matilda get ready for the storm, then took shelter with her when it hit. I hope Hob and Joseph are okay.* He rose to a sitting position, looked around. Yes, Matilda was sleeping on the other side of the shed. And there was the door.

He opened the door as quietly as he could. Outside, it was early morning. The ground was wet, and covered with leaves and branches. Where the sun reached, droplets of water sparkled. Gingerly, he stepped out and went to the horse-stalls. Hob and Joseph were sleeping curled up on hay, under horse blankets. The horses were awake, but drowsy. Off to one side he could hear the small river flowing, much louder than before with all the night's rainfall. The big river was only slightly higher—it would take time for the full storm-water to make its way there.

Over by the tavern, Tony was straightening things out. Benedict wandered off in his direction. "Hello, Benedict!" the tavern-keeper cried. "Could you help me get this canvas fly back up?"

Benedict helped with the ropes as Tony tied knots to hold the fly in place above the log sections that served him as tables. "How did you do over the night?" Benedict asked.

"No trouble at all. This wagon and I have gone through worse storms than this. I hope everything went as well at my inn in

Milltown. Should be okay, Maude was there to take care of it, and she had our daughter to help." Tony took dry firewood out of the wagon, started a small fire, and began heating a kettle of cider. People would want a warm drink, first thing off, and his livelihood came from satisfying that sort of want.

Once it was warm, Benedict purchased a small bucket of cider, the loan of some cups, and a large loaf of bread. He took them back to the paddock, and roused Hob and Joseph. He gave them cups of cider. "Here. Warm your bones." He left half the loaf of bread with them, and went into the shed.

Matilda was awake, and looking muzzily about. He set a cup of cider before her, then sat back to drink some himself. He tore off a piece of bread, and dipped it in his cup. Benedict didn't have the best teeth in Northlanding, and liked his food soft. His cook was wonderful with soups and stews.

Once Matilda was more awake, he smiled at her. "You came through the storm fine. I've been out checking. Your hay is a bit blown about, and there are stray branches in the paddock, but that's it." She smiled back.

"After we've had a bit to eat, and relieved ourselves, we can all work together to get things cleaned up." Benedict was definitely thinking of moving his horses in with Matilda for the rest of the Fair.

Ragnar Forkbeard was up also, and had roused his men. Everybody had slept fully-clothed, just in case. Dirk Cachepol was sleeping near his bed, and Ragnar nudged him into wakefulness. "It looks like the storm is over."

There was water on the floor, where a branch had poked through the canvas roof. There weren't any goods there, and the men in that area had wriggled aside in their sleep. No harm caused, just a bit of annoyance.

When they opened the door, there was a considerably larger branch waiting for them. "It's lucky *that* one missed," Dirk said.

"That's something you don't have to worry about in a storm at sea," Ragnar replied. "I think I'll go check the boats."

Ragnar sniffed the air. With all the traders, the fairgrounds had started to smell—inhabited. Now the air was clean again.

Oh, he could smell the wet ashes from yesterday's cook-fire, but that was a small thing.

Dirk looked over at the tavern, and saw Tony heating up cider. *It's time to repay hospitality,* Dirk thought. He hunted up a bucket in the booth, then went over to the tavern to get some cider.

When he got back, several men had taken dry wood out of the booth, and were helping Gunnar set up a fire to cook the barley-mash porridge he'd promised the night before. Others were chopping up the fallen branch to add to the fire once it got going. Still others were cleaning up the area. He offered the cider to them.

Ragnar returned from his inspection, and went over to Olaf's booth. He heard cursing from inside. He opened the door, stuck his head in. This roof had leaked too, over a stack of brocades. Olaf had covered them up with a bearskin, so the brocades were only a bit damp, but the bearskin needed serious cleaning before it could be sold. "What, more troubles?" Ragnar asked.

"It's not that bad. But we're going to have to patch the roof, and that was an exceptionally fine bearskin."

"At least the boats weathered the storm," Ragnar said. "We need to mend some canvas and do some bailing, but nothing serious. And Gunnar is starting breakfast."

Olaf came outside to look. "Praise Gunnar, because Tony seems busy right now." The tavernkeeper's wagon was besieged by merchants who were too busy cleaning up to cook breakfast. He was struggling to deal with them all.

"I'll wager his prices are higher this morning, too."

"I don't take bets like that," Olaf replied.

Olaf's men had come out of the booth, and were starting to set up frames for displaying cloth and drying the bearskin. Ragnar's men were putting out the display tables, and one was standing on another's shoulders to get the branch out of the hole in the roof and down to the ground.

"Give it a chance to dry before we try to patch that," Ragnar spoke in the carrying voice he used at sea.

Dirk came up, chewing on bread and drinking cider. "I have to get back to Northlanding, and find out what happened with the bailiff and the highwaymen."

"Travel well."

Dirk went over to Matilda's to collect his horse, and headed off down the road.

"You let him stay with you in the storm?" Olaf asked with a raised eyebrow.

"It can't hurt to shelter him, and it might make him more favorable toward us," Ragnar replied. "We may need favor. Gunnar had a vision last night, of the raven of death circling over us. I don't think the vision was about the storm."

When Dirk reached the castle, and gave his horse over to a servant, he was glad to see Gervase and four troopers on the muddy ground outside the keep. He went over to them. "It looks like you lived through yesterday." Then he noticed with a hitch of his throat that one trooper was missing. "Where's Thomas?"

Gervase saw Dirk's flinch as he looked over the men. "Thomas hurt his hip when his horse threw him during an ambush," the bailiff said. "He should be getting back to light work in a week or two. We killed two of the robbers outright, a third died last night, and one was hamstrung. I'd say we got off lightly."

"Did we find out anything useful?"

"Well, there don't seem to be any more highwaymen where those came from. But I don't think they had anything to do with Thorolf Pike."

"We need to talk about that."

The two men went to the center of the courtyard, where they weren't likely to be overheard. Dirk spoke first. "At the tavern, I learned a Finn saw Otkel putting up a rune-pole near where Thorolf was killed, on the day of his death."

"Hm," said Gervase.

"Ragnar and I, and four guards I borrowed from a merchant, went and got the pole and took it to the Northmen's sacred grove. The priest there read the runes and said they were poorly done. He thought they were meant to draw wealth, but they could just as well have cursed half the merchants in Northlanding."

"That doesn't sound good. I was talking with Otkel, and he told me of a brooch. He says if Ragnar has it, the only way he could have gotten it was off of Thorolf's body."

"So both of us spent time with our suspects? When the storm hit, I took shelter with Ragnar."

"Otkel helped me get the bandits' camp-goods back to the keep before the storm. I gave him shelter when it hit." Gervase chuckled. "He was trying very hard to convince me Ragnar was the killer. But I know enough to check everything Otkel says, before I believe it."

Dirk grinned a stubbly grin. "If he told me his cat ate a mouse, I'd go interview the local owls to see if they'd eaten that mouse instead. Or if, perhaps, they were missing a mouse they were saving for dinner."

"So, Dirk. What stories was Ragnar telling you?"

"Travel and trade, mostly. Storms on the sea. Only a few stories about Thorolf or Otkel."

"Well, either he has a clean conscience or he's being very cautious and quiet. Which did you think?"

"I think he has a clean conscience. But Thorolf and his men are outlawed from Surtsheim, so the laws of the Northmen would let him kill them with a clean conscience."

"Tell me again about those three boatloads of rich cargo and suspects, Dirk."

Dirk sighed. "I think we have to balance them against the warehouse of goods that Otkel and his Northmen are living in."

The bailiff sighed in return. "*I* think we should do what Otkel suggested. Ragnar Forkbeard may have a brooch that he took from Thorolf Pike, who six years ago took it from the body of Snorri Crow."

"Northmen are fond of genealogy, but I didn't know they used it for their possessions too, except maybe for swords."

"It matters here. Otkel suggests that Ragnar may have killed Thorolf, just so he could claim the brooch and return it to Snorri's family. That sounds unfortunately like the way Northmen handle their grudges.

"Be it as it may," Gervase continued, "it would be useful to know if Ragnar has the brooch. Otkel suggests Ragnar may have taken the King's Deer, and served it up for the noon meal day before yesterday. I can testify they had venison stew, and where else would they get the venison?"

"They had big stores of jerky, m'lud. They could have made stew from that."

"Oh, for Heaven's sake, Dirk. I don't think he actually *took* a deer, but it's a fine excuse for searching his camp without raising his hackles."

"Let's send a couple troopers with the gamekeeper, just to give us eyes and ears of our own on the scene."

"I can see that," the bailiff agreed. "Now what I think we should do, I'll get Otkel off to discuss the brooch while you talk with his men. See if Otkel was missing the evening Thorolf was killed, that sort of thing. And we'd better hurry, because they'll head for the fairgrounds soon to start doing as much trading as they can."

Gervase and Dirk detailed the two healthiest troopers to fetch the gamekeeper and bring him over to Otkel's, and told the others to rest. Then the bailiff and his deputy set out on foot for Thorolf's warehouse, no, *Otkel's* warehouse.

A servant let them in the gate, and went to inform Otkel. Then he returned, and took the bailiff and his deputy up to the greathall. It smelled of food, and servants were clearing away bowls and spoons. Otkel and eleven men were there, all dressed for trade and looking ready to head out for the fair. Starkad was wrapped up in blankets, coughing and shivering.

Gervase went over to Otkel and took him to one side. "I need your help for a short while. You should describe that brooch to the gamekeeper so he'll recognize it if he sees it."

Otkel turned to his men. "Load the alum, then take it to the shop of Samuel the dyer. Get a receipt from his people, and bring it to the fair," he told two of them. He looked to the rest. "Load up good samples of spices, cypress wood, and anything else you think people might want. Today, by Odin, we are going to make trades." Then he and the bailiff left.

Dirk looked over at Starkad. "He seems to have caught a fever at the fair. Do you think it was from Olaf throwing him in the water?"

"Oh, it could have been," Hermund said. "But Otkel had him running an errand in the storm. It's probably that."

"Isn't *that* just like the man in charge. They laze about like lords, and leave their men to do the nasty stuff. The bailiff sticks me with the footwork every time."

"You've got that right," Starkad croaked. "When we were hauling the goods from our first day at the fair, when Thorolf was still alive, we couldn't find hide nor hair of Otkel to help." He bent double with coughing.

"Let's not tell Otkel *or* the bailiff we feel that way," Dirk grinned. Everybody laughed, and they trooped down into the warehouse to begin the day's work.

The fairgrounds had been straightened out as much as possible. A few of the tents and pavilions had blown over. One had belonged to the copper merchant from across the sea, and while it was a nuisance, his cargo wasn't the least bit harmed. He'd done some trading in the previous days, but it was mostly for iron and well-packed glass, which water wouldn't hurt.

Other merchants had more delicate merchandise. Today, there would be bargain-sales for damaged wares. Most of the cloth merchants and the like, whose goods could be ruined by rain, had doubly-sturdy pavilions and had come through the storm well.

The sun had begun to bake the mud back into something solid. Ragnar's goods were on display, though he wore plainer clothing and boots than usual. He'd had a few tentative bargaining sessions, mostly with merchants working out of booths rather than tents.

He saw Otkel and his men approaching up the Northlanding road, leading pack-horses covered with goods. *It looks like he's ready to trade,* Ragnar thought. And sure enough, they went right over to Samuel the dyer. Otkel showed Samuel a scrap of parchment, and Samuel reluctantly went to his stores and handed over a large box of something. Otkel looked inside, smiled and nodded, and shook Samuel's hand. Then Otkel and his men moved on.

"It looks like Otkel is reduced to honest trade," Olaf said from behind.

"He and Thorolf always did give value for value received," Ragnar replied. "But their deals were harsh. That dyer didn't look happy. I suspect he barely broke even on the trade, whatever it was."

Ragnar watched Otkel and his men make the rounds. They seemed to be concentrating on the local merchants. *He must be trying to pick up momentum from people who are used to giving him deals,* Ragnar thought. *He can bargain with them any time. I wonder when he'll start leaning on outland traders? Still, Otkel seems to have some good merchandise. Maybe they have some decent spices? It might be worth it just to see Otkel's face if I offered to trade with him.*

John Freemantle came up then, bearing samples of wool. Ragnar hailed him. "John! I hope you spent the night well!"

John smiled. "The abbey walls are good, and the roof even better. And we managed to get our sheep under cover, so even freshly-sheared they weren't harmed by the storm. Now, about the wool...."

"Olaf wants wool, and I want some too. We need warm clothes on our steadings up north. And what do *you* seek?"

"We need shears. Our flocks keep growing, and more shears would help us deal with them. And Sister Katherine, in charge of our meals, admired the eating knife you gave me. She wonders if you have more, but less elaborate and expensive."

"The knives are easy." Ragnar lifted a chest onto the display table. "These are less expensive. Look them over."

While John was examining the knives, Ragnar saw three men approaching from the direction of Northlanding. When they were closer, he recognized two of the bailiff's troopers. The third was a stranger. As they approached his display, a pleasant scent of autumn herbs came from the troopers, especially noticeable in the morning's clean air.

"May I help you, good gentles?" he asked them.

"I'm the gamekeeper for Northlanding," the stranger introduced himself, "and there are rumors you have taken the King's Deer. I'd like to check your area to see if there's any evidence of that."

"Why, of course! I'll not stand in your way. Our cooking area is between my booth and the next." Ragnar's stomach sank. *Did somebody see that deer? I hope Gunnar disposed of the remains as well as he said.*

Gunnar was adding dried peas to the stewpot when he looked up and saw three men coming his way. A raven was flying above them.

"The raven," he whispered.

Chapter 12
Wednesday: Evidences

"You are Gunnar, the cook for this encampment?"

"I am. And who might you be?" Gunnar asked. A raven croaked in the tree above, which had one branch fewer than before the storm.

"I'm the gamekeeper for Northlanding, and I've heard that somebody took one of the King's Deer and gave it to you to cook."

Hel take that deer, Gunnar thought. *At least it tasted good. And I cleaned up very well, after I prepared it.* "Why, I brought plenty of jerky. I know how fussy your king is about his deer. But Northmen do love their venison."

"I hope you don't mind if I look around," the gamekeeper said. "I brought some troopers to keep me honest." He waved his hand to indicate the bailiff's men.

"I've met those troopers," Gunnar replied. "I even gave one of the bailiff's men some of the stew. But he isn't with you."

One of the troopers snickered. "He's back at the castle, recovering from the stew."

Gunnar could have taken that as an insult, but decided it was testimony to the accuracy of his aim. He smiled. "I thought it hit the spot for him. Perhaps he had too much."

The gamekeeper shook his head. The cook and the troopers were talking right past him, and he didn't like it. He jerked his thumb at the troopers. "Get to it, and see what you can find." The three began searching around the firepit and the cauldron. Gunnar stood back, crossed his arms, and let them.

They checked the ground, spiraling out from the firepit, and examined the branches of the tree to see if anything had been hung from it. It was damaged from the storm, and what might have happened before that was unclear. Then they began looking under the seating-logs. "Pay attention, men, things accumulate in places like this," the gamekeeper instructed the troopers.

One trooper lifted his lip and whispered to the other. "Teach your grandmother how to suck eggs while you're at it."

The gamekeeper reached under one log, and pulled out a chunk of antler. He held it up to Gunnar, and raised his eyebrow.

Gunnar came over, and looked at the piece. "You're a gamekeeper. You know perfectly well that's a piece of mature antler. Where are we going to find a deer with mature antlers this time of year? We *sell* antler. If you want more, there's a large pile of moose antler in the booth."

Chastened, the gamekeeper went back to work. One trooper found a tarnished silver penny, then the other found a spoon, and a rusty nail. Finally the gamekeeper dug under a log with a stick, and pulled out an elaborate brooch. He rubbed it partly clean with a cloth, and held it up. "Somebody was careless." He held it up, giving everybody a chance to see the brooch. "But this certainly is handsome." Gold, silver, and copper animals gleamed from the high points he'd cleaned.

Gunnar examined it. "Wait a moment. That's Snorri Crow's brooch. It's famous. How did you find it under there?"

"I dug with a stick."

"That brooch should go to Snorri Crow's family. It's part of his son's heritage." Gunnar reached for it.

One of the troopers got to it first. "The bailiff has been looking for this brooch. He thinks it might be important evidence." He held it closely, fended off Gunnar's hand. Gunnar wasn't ready to get forcible with a lawman, so the trooper kept it.

The search for the King's Deer died out from lack of interest. The gamekeeper and troopers looked around a few moments longer, but soon left.

Ragnar Forkbeard and John Freemantle had stepped to one side as the gamekeeper and troopers headed back toward Gunnar and the cooking area. After that, Ragnar wasn't talkative.

John noticed, and tried to fill in the gap. "It seems Abbess Margaret's salve is getting some use beyond the abbey walls."

Ragnar looked at John in an inquiring manner.

"It was those troopers. I could smell the salve on them. Nothing quite like it."

"What's it good for?" Ragnar asked.

"Rashes, poison ivy, itching, things like that. It's not a perfect healer, but it can be a comfort."

"Does it work on mosquito bites? Surtsheim is full of thirsty mosquitoes."

"It might," John said. "Are you thinking you want some?"

"I'd have to talk with Abbess Margaret to be sure, but it sounds useful. Perhaps you could trade some for those knives you're looking at?"

"We'll both have to talk with the Abbess, but that's the kind of trade she would approve."

Ragnar, who'd kept an ear turned in Gunnar's direction, heard him fussing about Snorri Crow's brooch. "That sounds like trouble. I should be somewhere else when those troopers come back out. If I disappear, could you have Abbess Margaret, or perhaps Father Hugh, ask the bailiff if he happens to have me somewhere about his dungeon?" He beckoned to Knute, pointed at the display tables, and as Knute came to take over the trading, Ragnar quickly headed to Olaf Far-traveler's booth.

"Olaf, I think somebody is trying to get me arrested for Thorolf's killing. I'm going to make myself scarce. Watch over the booths, could you?" And he walked off, taking a crooked path among the merchants' areas.

Ragnar ended up at James Smith's forge, where he could watch both his booth and the Northlanding road. "Ready to do some trading?" James asked.

"No, I'm avoiding trouble. I think Otkel is planting evidence on me, trying to get me arrested over this Thorolf thing. I may have to head back up-river sooner than I expected. And if that happens, I don't know as I'll be coming back next year."

James seemed shaken. "That's terrible news! I'll miss visiting with you, and I use a lot of that good Surtsheim iron you bring."

"If you wake up tomorrow morning and find a pile of iron where my boat is today, take the iron and work out a decent bargain with Olaf. If you can't use it all, turn the rest over to Benedict. He can trade it off and get the silver to me. If we're rowing upriver, I won't want the weight."

Smithies are dark, so the smith can better judge the glow of the iron. From the dimness, unseen, Ragnar could see his booth. He watched the gamekeeper and the troopers questioning Knute, John, and Olaf. They eventually left, seeming dissatisfied, and headed down the Northlanding road.

James headed over to the road, and checked. Then he came back. "They seem to be truly gone." Ragnar clapped James' shoulder, and walked back to his booth. James watched unhappily as Ragnar went. He slammed the side of his fist down on the anvil, and cursed under his breath.

When Ragnar reached the booths, John, Olaf, Gunnar, Knute, Atli, and Ari gathered around him. They all went back to the cooking area, where they'd be less visible. "What were those three doing here?" Ragnar asked. "I don't think it was about the King's Deer."

Gunnar pointed at the logs. "They dug around under there, and came up with Snorri Crow's brooch, the one that went missing after he was killed. The one we think Thorolf took."

"I am getting very tired of Thorolf," Ragnar said. "And now somebody has planted that brooch on us. If Thorolf took it six years ago, and we turned up with it now, that would be strong evidence against us. As best I can tell, the bailiff seems to have decided it's either me or Otkel did the deed."

Gunnar folded his arms. "That gamekeeper didn't plant the brooch. I was watching, and he really did dig it out from under the log. But it wasn't tarnished, so it hadn't been there long. And the troopers said the bailiff was looking for just such a brooch."

"Loki take an interest in those troopers, and whoever put the brooch there as well!"

Ragnar tugged for a while on his beard as he thought. "Here's what we have to do. Keep trading, but inside our booth, get everything ready for us to leave tonight. It's still morning. I'm going to get to the bottom of this today, by Thor. If I can't, we'll be gone tomorrow morning and the bailiff can whistle for us. Olaf can stay and finish up his deals, because I'm pretty sure they're just looking at me."

Ragnar assigned his son Knute to take care of the booth and the trading. He had been talking with Gunnar in the cooking circle, until Ragnar arrived. Then Ragnar took Ari and Atli with him, and they headed over to the paddock. Both Matilda and Benedict had horses there, and they got the three fastest horses available.

Ragnar mounted up. "I want to see where Thorolf was killed." And they rode off toward Northlanding.

It wasn't long before they reached the place the body was found. Atli and Ari had been there, watching things while the bailiff was investigating. He showed Ragnar where the body was, and the polearm. And he pointed out the underbrush where Gervase thought the arrow had come from. Ragnar looked at the underbrush. "Let's see if the rain has turned anything up since the troopers searched," Ragnar said. He started to step into the bushes, but halted.

"Atli, did the troopers seem unhappy about searching here?"

"They did, but the bailiff spoke sharply to them, and they went in."

"Do you suppose Gervase Rotour has poor sight at a distance?"

Ari said he'd heard that. "Dirk recognized Otkel and the other Northmen long before Gervase did."

Ragnar laughed. "And here we are, right by the Abbey Road. Let's go pay Abbess Margaret a visit. I have a hunch to check out."

When the troopers and the gamekeeper got back to the keep, they turned the brooch over to the bailiff. "There wasn't any evidence of poaching, but the brooch was under one of the logs near the fire circle."

Gervase moved the brooch around to look at it from all directions. "That's a peculiar place to lose something this valuable."

"Oh, there were other things." They showed him a tarnished silver coin, a rusted nail, a bronze ring, and a spoon. "People lose stuff when they're sitting, paying attention to something else. And if I feared a search, that could be a good place to hide valuables."

Gervase cleaned the brooch more thoroughly. It had no rust or tarnish. It hadn't been lying there for years, like the nail and the coin. "This is a pretty pickle. That cook identified the brooch as Snorri Crow's, you say? It's strong evidence, but not strong enough to make me want to stir up thirty Northmen who might object to our taking Ragnar Forkbeard away. And who knows what the other traders from the north would think of it all?"

"It's even better," Dirk replied. "Otkel had Starkad out in the storm, running an errand. He's back at their warehouse, coughing his lungs out. It must have been quite an errand."

"This is getting ridiculous. Starkad is sick, and the others are at the fair? Get our physician over to tend to Starkad. I owe Otkel and his men a favor for helping me with those highwaymen, after all. Some tincture of poppy should help his cough, and perhaps loosen his tongue. I want to find out what that errand was. You find out from Starkad, I'll find out from Otkel, and then we'll compare their tales."

Dirk went to the physician's room. They packed some healing medicines, and went off to the warehouse. Gervase saddled a horse and headed for the fair. *My horse is dead,* he grumbled to himself. *Not only do I have to chase all over, I have to do it on a strange horse.*

At the warehouse, Dirk knocked on the door. A servant led them up to the greathall where Starkad was alone, wrapped in a blanket, shivering and coughing. "I've brought you our physician," Dirk told him. "You helped with the bandits yesterday, and we want to return the favor."

The physician listened to Starkad's lungs, and rapped his chest, then had Starkad urinate in a flask and examined the urine. "I don't think you're in danger," he told Starkad. "But you're in for an unpleasant week or so." He took out a bottle of medicine, removed the stopper, poured some into a very small cup. "Drink this." He handed it to Starkad. "It should ease your cough, and maybe cool your fever a bit." Starkad made a face at the strong taste, but drank it all down.

They sat for a while in the still dimness of the hall, chatting. Starkad soon was more relaxed, and coughing less terribly. "I'll leave you some of the medicine," the physician said. "It might be best for you to rest in the solar, with the door closed. You'll have a more peaceful time of it, and so will the others. Above all, don't go out in the rain for at least two weeks. You might relapse."

Dirk smiled sympathetically. "Trust him. Physicians know about going out in unpleasant weather."

"We have to. It's our duty to help the sick, even when the weather is bad."

Dirk shivered a bit. "I know. And sometimes I have to go out when the lawbreakers are indoors hiding from the weather." He was silent for a moment, then looked at Starkad. "What the devil got you outdoors during that storm?"

Starkad bent over coughing. His shoulders twitched with the effort. "Otkel had to get a message to Samuel the dyer. I stayed at his shop afterwards, until the morning after the storm broke." He leaned back, and closed his eyes. Since Dirk had asked his question, Starkad hadn't looked straight at him.

Dirk took Starkad by the shoulder. "Get better, man. One of these days, we'll all have to become lords or great merchants so we can tell *other* people to go out in the rain."

"I'll leave the medicine, and the cup, with you," the physician said. "No more than four cups spread out over a day, mind you, and stop taking it once you feel better. This isn't a safe medicine to take for a long time. It helps you master the cough, but if you take too much, too long, the medicine will end up mastering *you*. I'll be back in a week or so to get what's left."

Outside the warehouse, Dirk and the physician headed back to the castle keep. But once they were well away, Dirk told the physician to go to the keep by himself. "Me, I'm going to pay a visit to Samuel the dyer's shop." He turned left, and headed towards the downwind side of town, where the dyers and the tanners worked.

Otkel was having better success at the fair this day. On the inside, he was eating his liver out because the deals weren't as good as Thorolf could have gotten—but at least he was making deals. He traded spices to the copper merchant in return for blue vitriol, then traded the vitriol to the man with the alum to more than recoup the amount he gave the dyer.

One of the woodworkers inquired about the cypress wood. "It's very handsome. What are its virtues?"

"It doesn't rot," Otkel told him. "It makes great tool handles, and if you use it for the legs of chairs and chests, they stay sound even if the floor is damp." The woodworker had had problems with damp during the storm, and he liked the idea of cypress. He offered many little carved and decorated boxes in exchange. Otkel needed more cypress to make up the deal, so he sent one of his men back to the warehouse with the horseload of alum, to return with cypress.

Then Otkel decided it was time to talk with James Smith. He went over to the smithy, and looked over the merchandise. There was a handsome array of swords, axes, and hatchets, nicely polished, gleaming in the sun. His men crowded around behind him. They all appreciated a good sword. "I see you have quite a few of your new swords, James."

"Yes," James replied. "I'd like to thank you for helping spread around the news."

"I'm sure you'll be willing to let us have some swords at the same price as before."

"I'm not so agreeable to that," James replied as he shook his head. "Thorolf was famous and powerful. His name alone sold things. While I'm sure you're a good merchant, so am I. I'd like to try doing my own deals. You and Thorolf made quite a profit with my swords, but they're well known now. I think I can do business without your help."

Otkel fumed. *This one's going to be tough,* he thought. But he gave a strained smile to James. "Don't forget, we offer you our protection as well as our services as merchants. Who knows what might happen without protection?"

James dropped his pleasant demeanor. The banked coals of his forge glowed red behind him, and wisps of smoke drifted past his face. He raised his hammer in one great sooty hand, and pointed with it to Matilda's paddock. Matilda and Benedict were there, watching, and a number of merchants' guards were standing idly by. Several of Ragnar and Olaf's Northmen were strolling about.

Otkel snarled in the back of his mind. *Loki seize these busybodies,* he thought. His hand twitched toward the axe over his shoulder, but he restrained it. James had a hammer in his grasp, and smiths are among the strongest of men. He was silent for a moment, then spoke in a low and deadly voice. "You make a good argument, James. For your sake, I hope it is enough to comfort you when you are back at home in Northlanding."

Then Otkel and his men departed. But they all knew that threatening Matilda the other day had cost them dearly, both from lost goodwill and lost fearsomeness.

"It might be wise to show everybody there's no hard feelings over yesterday." Otkel led the way over to Olaf's booth, and examined his displays. "You have some very fine cloth," he told Olaf. "Is there anything you might want in trade for it?"

"I've heard you have cinnamon and vanilla beans. My wife Aud cooks twice as well when she has spices to work with."

"We have cinnamon and vanilla, tea from the east, cardamom, black pepper, and salt. Perhaps you'd like some dried red peppers? The Skraelings to the southwest say they warm up your blood. In the cold North, you might appreciate that. I certainly do here in Northlanding."

One of Otkel's men got some spices from a packhorse, and Otkel handed them to Olaf. While Olaf was sniffing and tasting, Otkel looked around. There was a bearskin drying on an improvised rack. He could smell the damp fur.

"Did one of your bearskins get damaged in the storm? It looks wet."

Olaf snorted, and jerked his thumb backwards toward his booth. "A branch fell and poked a hole in our roof. I used the bearskin to protect the brocades. It's a lot easier to clean bearskins." He went back to tasting spices.

"It's a bother to clean hides in the middle of a fair, and until it's cleaned it's damaged goods. You could sell us the skin at a discount, and let us do the work of cleaning?"

Olaf looked at Otkel, eyes and nose streaming. "Are you sure these red peppers are okay? Are they supposed to do this?" Then the two set out on a discussion of bearskins and spices, brocade and cypress. *By all the gods, I'm going to skin that bastard on this trade,* they both thought. But they were too evenly matched as merchants. In the end, the only skin involved had once belonged to a bear.

Otkel gave his spices over to Olaf, and silver as well, and his men began loading brocade onto packhorses. They covered the brocade over with the bearskin, to keep it from the dirt of the road, which was still damp enough that horses' hooves could splatter mud. "We'll send a horse back to bring you the cypress, and the rest of the spices."

Otkel and the men went over to the tavern, where Otkel gave silver to Tony, the tavernkeeper. "That bargaining was thirsty work. Bring us ale."

"Can I have some too?" came a voice from behind. Otkel turned, and there was Gervase.

This could be good or bad, Otkel thought. "Good day, lord Bailiff. How is your visit to the fair going?" He stretched his hand out to the stump next to him. "Sit, sit. Join us."

"I'm still searching everywhere to find who killed Thorolf," the bailiff replied. "And I have troopers checking things out in Northlanding." Gervase looked at the packhorses with admiration. "You seem to be doing good trades.

"You should know, your man Starkad was doing very poorly after you left. I sent over our physician with some of his finest medicines, and Starkad is much better now. The physician says it might be wise for him to rest in the solar, where his coughing won't bother the rest of your men."

Otkel nodded. "That sounds like a good idea. I'll certainly arrange that."

Gervase took a long draw from his mug of ale. "What the devil was so important you had to send Starkad out in weather like that?"

Otkel flinched inside. "It was *his* errand – he didn't tell me what he was about."

Gervase shook his head. "Foolish, foolish man!" He raised his hand to catch Tony's eye. "Bread!" he called, as he waved a silver penny. Tony brought two loaves over, and Gervase and the men began to tear them apart and eat. Otkel didn't appear hungry. He went straight back to his ale, instead.

Chapter 13
Wednesday: Decisions

The shadowed corridor of elms leading to the abbey was even greener than before the storm, but leaves and branches, small and large, lay scattered about. Most of the large ones had been moved to the side, but there was still work to be done. The horses' hooves were quiet on the soft, damp ground. "Stay with the horses when we get there," Ragnar said to Ari and Atli as they rode. "I have careful talking to do. The fewer people there are, the less complicated it will be."

Rather than the chaos of his last visit, the abbey pasturelands were dotted with fresh-sheared sheep and a few shepherds. The peasants, who'd been so busy with the shearing, were in the distance working their field strips. The three Northmen dismounted at the gatehouse. The brothers stayed to watch the horses, while Ragnar spoke with the gatekeeper. "I'm here to talk with Abbess Margaret or Father Hugh."

"That's a surprise," the old man replied. "John Freemantle went to the fair to talk with *you*."

"John and I were bargaining over the Abbess' soothing salve. He told me I should really talk with *her* to learn what it works for. I was nearby on another errand, and decided to do so."

"That makes a lot of sense," the gatekeeper nodded. He summoned a messenger. Then he pointed to the bench beneath the oak, near the gates of the cloister. "She'll meet you there."

Ragnar sat on the bench, enjoyed the air and shade, and waited. In a few moments Abbess Margaret and Father Hugh came toward him. The Abbess bore a towel and a basin, and she washed his hands when she reached him. "Here again so soon after your last visit, Master Ragnar?"

> If you have friends you fully trust
> Go often to their house.
> Grass and brambles surely grow
> On the untrodden path.

"My friends, it's good to see you again. But I had other matters in mind when I made this visit."

"Oh?" asked the Abbess as she raised her brows.

"John Freemantle and I were speaking of that salve you make. I was wondering if you could tell me of its virtues."

The Abbess was quiet in thought a moment. "It's a new medicine. We've been sending out missionaries to the Skraelings, and one of their medicine men gave us the recipe in exchange for a steel hatchet. He said it was good against itching and hives and poison ivy, very good against mosquito-bite, and almost useless against wasp and bee stings."

"I needed some the other day," Father Hugh added. "It worked very well."

"My homeland is filled with mosquitoes and biting flies. I should take salve back with me."

"I don't have much now," Abbess Margaret said. "And I can't make more until late summer when the herbs are grown. But I can give you some to try." She sent the messenger to get a pot. "Next year, you'll know how much you want, and I'll have more experience making it. We can talk trade then."

"Lady Margaret, this is more generous than I hoped. Tell me, who have you given the salve to? I can ask them how it worked for them."

The Abbess thought a moment. "Except for using it here at the Abbey, I've only given it to the baron's physician to try out."

Father Hugh raised his head. "James Smith came by with a poison-ivy rash, asking if we had any remedy. I gave him some, too. It didn't seem worth bothering you over that."

The messenger returned with a small earthenware pot, covered with parchment tied in place. Ragnar took it. "Thank you, Abbess Margaret. Thank you, Father Hugh. Now I know who to talk to besides yourselves. The fair continues, I must return, but you both have my gratitude." He rose, clasped Father Hugh's hand, bowed to the Abbess, then went toward the gatehouse.

Ragnar mounted his horse, and so did Ari and Atli. They rode back beneath the trees.

"I think we should go talk with James Smith," Ragnar said to his men.

* * *

After his short visit to the Fair, Gervase rode back to the castle. He'd had his talk with Otkel. Now he needed to check Otkel's words against Starkad's. He dismounted and gave his horse into the care of a stableman.

Dirk was waiting in the keep, busying himself with sausage and ale. "Starkad's tale didn't check out. He told me Otkel had him carry a message to Samuel the dyer. But neither Samuel nor his men saw Starkad, nor received a message through him."

The bailiff shook his head. "That's not Otkel's story. He says it was a personal errand of Starkad's, and Starkad didn't tell him what it was about. A fine mess, hm? Well, at least we have that brooch from out by Ragnar's booth."

"I wouldn't rely on that brooch. I was with Ragnar during that storm, and we couldn't have heard a squad of excited horsemen outside. We should find exactly what Starkad *was* doing, now that we know some things he wasn't."

"Dirk, get the troopers and bring them up to my quarters. It's time to pull together everything we know, and see if it makes a picture."

Soon enough all seven men were there, Gervase and Dirk and five troopers. One trooper used a crutch. Gervase and Dirk talked of Otkel and Starkad and errands in the storm. Then Gervase held up the brooch. "Otkel told me Thorolf took this brooch from Snorri Crow six years ago, and that Ragnar might well kill Thorolf to reclaim the brooch for Snorri's family. Just this morning, two of you and the gamekeeper found this out by Ragnar's cooking fire. That's suspicious – almost as suspicious as Starkad's errand, hm?"

"We had to dig it out of the ground," a trooper noted.

"Wait a minute," Rhys said. "I saw that brooch in Otkel's greathall after Thorolf's pyre. I was with him, and went to the feast in honor of Thorolf's memory. Otkel chopped open Thorolf's treasure-chest, and was giving gifts. That brooch was right on top of the pile when they poured the chest out. It's so handsome, I couldn't miss it."

"That's enough!" Gervase roared as he slammed his fist down on the desk. "I've had it up to *here* with Otkel. First Starkad has an ill-explained mission out in the storm, then the day after the storm this brooch turns up at Ragnar's camp. I don't think it walked there by itself, and it's no hard guess whose feet carried it. *Nobody* gets away with planting evidence to fool me."

"Come dawn, when Otkel and all of his men are at their warehouse, I want to ask them some very pointed questions. Sharpen your points and sleep well tonight, men, and don't talk to anybody. We're getting up early tomorrow to give Otkel a surprise."

Dirk rubbed his stubbly jaw with a rasping sound. "Otkel shot an arrow in the air. I hope he's happy with where it comes down."

At the fair, Ragnar and his men dismounted at the paddock, then walked to James Smith's small blacksmith shop. They heard the clangor of an anvil, but it stopped when Ragnar hailed James out. Ragnar looked at all the passersby, then told James, "we must speak about your purchase of iron. Come with me to my ship."

Ragnar and James walked to the ship together, followed by Ari and Atli. But at the ship Ragnar continued walking upstream, drawing James along with him. They went until they were well out of earshot from the fair. The river was high from the storm, and made enough sound rippling over a fallen tree that they were safe from being overheard. The roar of the falls made speech doubly safe. The trees were green and lush after the rain. It was noon, so they shaded the four men.

"Your iron is in danger of being confiscated by the bailiff. He seems to think I killed Thorolf Pike, and your law takes the property of criminals. He may yet arrest me and seize my goods. I hold you at least partly responsible for this, as you killed Thorolf and then did not announce your deed."

James gaped.

"James, *somebody* had to have a reason for this killing. It was not robbery—Thorolf's purse was left, and the horse not stolen. All we men of Surtsheim had strong reason to kill Thorolf, and many of you local merchants were very worried about Thorolf encroaching on your operations.

"The arrow that killed Thorolf had a shaft of maple rather than pine, suggesting it was a local person. My men and I have pine arrow shafts, for maple is uncommon as far north as Surtsheim."

Ragnar held out the small jar of salve he'd gotten from Abbess Margaret, and wafted a bit of the odor at James. "This is a new medicine. I've smelled that salve only twice at the fair – once on you, once on the bailiff's troopers. And the bushes where the archer must have hidden to shoot Thorolf from ambush are filled with poison ivy."

James backed up, and bumped into Ari.

"The bailiff made his troopers go into those bushes to investigate, though Atli testifies they were reluctant. The Abbess says she only gave salve to the baronial physician, but Father Hugh says he gave some to you for poison ivy. There are many local merchants with reason to kill Thorolf – but only one local merchant with a case of poison ivy."

James gave in. "I tried to avoid the ivy. I must have brushed against some as I was leaving. It was late twilight by then, and hard to tell the plants. A good shot, considering the light. I can't say I regret it."

James paused a moment. "What are you going to do about this?"

Ragnar frowned. "None of us here will weep for Thorolf, but justice must be done. This is why secret murder is forbidden, James. It brings suspicion into peoples' minds. It's hard enough dealing with death, without adding suspicion. I'm at serious risk from your actions. Will you grant me judgement?"

"You? Only the king and his courts have the right to judge!"

"You're an Englishman. That's your way. I don't care about your king's opinion in this matter, and you seem willing to avoid his judgement. Among Northmen, judgements are made by the community assembled together at the Althing, unless agreement can be reached beforehand. Thorolf was a Northman, we are Northmen, and I am offering you the chance to be judged by our laws rather than yours."

James seemed to grasp the formality of the situation. He stood a moment in thought. "Then I will grant you judgement. You're an honorable man—and I'll probably get a less harsh judgement from you than I would from the Baron."

The three Northmen relaxed, took formal poses instead of wary ones.

"Very well, then," Ragnar said. "Thorolf was outlawed, so it is legal to kill him, but you did so secretly, which is itself a crime. I shall balance these two against one another, and rule this be counted as an ordinary killing.

"You had a good reason for the killing. Thorolf had been threatening tradesmen's families some years back, and it looked like he or Otkel might be starting again. Even without that, he'd been threatening you, your wife, and your son. I think most Northmen would agree the killing was justified.

"Thorolf was an important man in your community. Even for a justified killing, the compensation for such a man is two hundred ounces of silver. However, I have been at these trade fairs for years. It seems to me that Thorolf's practices have cost you at least that sum. I rule that he has collected his wergild himself, in advance, and you are quit of any claims against you.

"Since you have been judged as having satisfied the laws of Surtsheim District so far as I am concerned, there is no reason for me to further tax you with this killing, save that you help me escape the attentions of the bailiff. I rule that none of us speak of this judgement. The bailiff, the baron, and the king have no legitimate claim against you under the laws of Surtsheim."

Everybody there agreed that this should be so. Then Ari and Atli, as witnesses, repeated the words of the judgement, and they all grasped hands.

"I was careful asking questions once I suspected you," Ragnar said. "I don't think people will come bothering you over things I've said. But the bailiff seems determined to catch somebody. I want the bailiff to take a harder look at Otkel. It's only fair—Otkel used Snorri Crow's brooch to make the bailiff take a harder look at me. And Otkel's done enough other ill deeds that I'll not cry if something bad happens to him.

"James, you should ask the local merchants for stories of Otkel's ill deeds, and if you should find the bailiff is coming for me, you must notify me as rapidly as you can. I'm going to check with my men and Olaf's, also. Then I'm going to make a scorn poem."

"A poem?" James Smith was incredulous.

Ragnar smiled. "A Northman with a strong poem is very dangerous."

Chapter 14
Thursday: Things Collapse

Ragnar didn't rest much that night. He was turning ideas, words, and verses over in his mind. The weavings of his bed creaked softly as he rolled about. As he finally drifted toward sleep, he noticed Gunnar lighting his lantern from the coals in his small fire-carrier. Gunnar went out the door. There was a crackling noise as he started a fire in his cook-pit.

A hand on his shoulder shook Ragnar awake. He could smell porridge and broth. The door to the booth was open. There was the faintest hint of dawn in the East, and Gunnar was standing over him. "Let's rouse the men, and break our fast," Ragnar said. The two of them went about stirring people into wakefulness.

Ragnar and Gunnar were first to the food. As Gunnar was ladling out porridge, he spoke quietly. "A Valkyrie came to visit last night."

"Oh?"

"I'd started the fire, and was waiting for the water to heat. I noticed a tall, strong woman next to me, by that tree. She was armed, armored, richly dressed, and she moved like a warrior. She seemed very real, more real than most of us. I could hear a horse whickering nearby. 'Gunnar, you've waited long enough to settle matters with Otkel,' she told me. 'Today will pay for all.' Then she vanished into the shadows. I'd never seen her before."

Ragnar's brows rose, and he stroked his beard in thought. "That's a better omen than the raven you saw circling during the storm. Perhaps this whole problem will be taken care of today."

"For me, at least," Gunnar said. He looked very much like a man who'd been waiting to end a problem.

Ragnar had no reply to that. He sat and ate, and his men came grumbling sleepily out to join them. Some men came from the other booths, too: men that had no love for Thorolf, nor for Otkel. Eventually there were twenty. Olaf was among them.

As they were eating, Ragnar stood. "Somebody hid Snorri Crow's brooch here to make the bailiff suspicious. Only Thorolf—and then Otkel—would have had that brooch. Today, I speak to Otkel."

He looked to Olaf. "Olaf, this is my fight, and Gunnar's. I'd consider it a great favor if you stayed here with some men and kept our camp and possessions safe while we're gone."

Then he looked about. "They won't let us through the gate into Northlanding if we look like a war party. We all should put on our finest clothes. Bring weapons. If you want a mail shirt, wear it beneath your tunic. I'll carry a shield. Some of the things I'm going to say might make Otkel want to throw axes. He's known for that."

Everybody went back to their booths to prepare. Before the sun was up and the fairgrounds wakeful, they were walking toward Northlanding on the traders' road. Tony was already preparing his tavern for the coming day. He watched them leave.

Dirk Cachepol was snoring mightily when a night watchman carefully poked him awake. "The watch is changing, Dirk. You wanted to be roused then."

Dirk grunted and grumbled and rubbed his eyes. "What's the weather like?"

"A light breeze, no clouds, cool, and dawn just starting."

Dirk rolled upright. "Good. Today's going to be busy. At least it won't be hot or wet." He shoved his feet into boots, buttoned them up over his breeches, and shrugged into the padded gambeson he wore beneath armor. He lit a rushlight from the watchman's torch. Then he strolled into the barracks, and used the rushlight to ignite the candles in their sconces.

"Up and at 'em, men," he bellowed. Four troopers startled, twitched, or quietly opened their eyes into wakefulness. "Otkel doesn't know to wait for us, so if we're slow, he'll be gone to the fair. Get fed, use the jakes, then into your armor!" He clapped his hands. Servants brought in bread and ale.

The men were soon dressing as Dirk hustled them along. They put on padded gambesons, mail shirts over them, and steel caps on their heads. "We're one man short today, with Thomas wounded by those highwaymen. We'll all have to be extra sharp to make up for that. So wear the livery. This is an official visit to Otkel, after all. We want to look our very best, impressive and intimidating."

Dirk led the men out the gate of the keep onto the grounds, where the grass glistened with dew. They stood there in the earliest light of dawn. As soon as they'd lined up, the bailiff stepped out to join them.

Gervase was armed and armored much like the others, but in brown fabric of high quality. His mail was somewhat longer in the sleeve, and lightly browned to match the fabric. He also had a steel breastplate painted with the baronial coat of arms: a blue ground with green pines outlined in white on left and right. At the top was a white snowflake; at the bottom, a yellow ship-dock with details picked out in brown. He was wearing the sword he'd confiscated from the highwaymen two days earlier.

He began walking toward the castle gate. "Let's move out." The gate itself wasn't yet open for the day, but the gatekeeper unbarred a small door and let them out through that.

As they walked through the streets of town, the sun began to rise at their right. Its rays gleamed from the golden cross atop the cathedral. When they approached the merchants' quarter, street vendors were setting up their awnings, their brightly-colored carpets, and painted carts. "Apples, m'lords? Stored in caves, crisp as when they were picked!" Gervase shook his head 'no,' but Dirk took one and tossed the vendor a copper.

By the time they neared Otkel's warehouse, Dirk had finished the apple. He threw away the core. Almost before it stopped rolling, sparrows were squabbling over it. Gervase held up his hand to signal a halt.

"Men, we've all been to the warehouse. The south and west sides are up against other warehouses, so we don't have to worry much about them. The east side has small windows at street level, and they could slide down ropes from the windows in their greathall. The north side has the gate. I'm going up to the gate alone. The rest of you wait around the corner on the east side. Watch those windows! And keep an eye out that they don't escape from the solar's window onto the roof to the south."

They walked the rest of the way. Once his men were out of sight, Gervase went up to the gate. It was sturdy, thick-hewn planks girded with great iron straps and many, many iron nails. He reached out to the massive door-knocker, and brought it down once, twice, thrice. The sound echoed in the street.

Otkel and his men were well-dressed in preparation for the day's trading, and eating their breakfasts. Starkad had joined them from the solar, wrapped up in a blanket for warmth. He was still coughing, but not nearly as badly. "That medicine the physician gave me is really helping," he said in a voice somewhere between a croak and normal.

A loud knocking at the gate to his compound distracted them.

Soon one of the servants entered. "The bailiff is here, wishing to speak with you," he told Otkel.

"Why didn't you bring him up?"

"I looked through the speaking-hole. He was wearing armor, and carrying a sword."

"There's only one of him, and twelve of us. What danger could he be?" And then Otkel's eyes widened. "There *is* only one of him? Look out all the windows, and check!"

The servant rushed to the windows on the side wall, and looked out. "Dirk Cachepol and four troopers are waiting around the corner, with armor and swords. They saw me looking at them."

Otkel cursed. "We sacrificed plenty to Odin at Thorolf's pyre. He wouldn't forsake us. But with this much trouble, there must be *some* gods against us. That Ragnar, he sacrifices to Thor, *and* gets along with the priests of the White Christ. And I've never trusted that bailiff."

He fumed for a moment, then withdrew into calm. "Men, whatever you do, don't let them in." He went into his room and threw open the window. There the bailiff was on the street below, in full armor and livery. The rising sun reflected from his polished steel cap.

"I'm told you want to speak with me," Otkel said down to Gervase.

"Why, yes," the bailiff replied. "I was wondering if you could tell me how that brooch got from Thorolf's treasure-trove the night of his pyre, to Ragnar's camp at the fairgrounds yesterday morning."

"I'm sure I don't know what you mean," Otkel said. But he was thinking, *Hel take it, I knew it was bad having that Welsh trooper follow me around. He must have seen it in the trove.*

"I'm sure if you think hard you could come up with something."

The men were clustering around the door, listening as Otkel spoke. As one, they turned to look at Starkad, who coughed.

"I was with you most of the day, and night, of the storm," Otkel told the bailiff. "I couldn't have done it."

"Perhaps one of your men moved the brooch? I hear Starkad was out in the storm."

"I wouldn't know. If he was, that was his business. I certainly didn't tell him to do it."

Behind him, Starkad was quietly turning purple with rage. His scars stood out in strong contrast. He clenched his fist, held it quivering by his side. The others moved back.

Then Otkel saw motion, outside and to his right. He looked, and saw Ragnar Forkbeard coming down the street with twenty men. *Maybe I should have sacrificed the white bear furs,* Otkel thought. *This sure doesn't look like I have Odin's favor.* "We seem to have an interruption."

Ragnar and the men arrived in front of Thorolf's warehouse. It was a strong timbered building, with a walled yard and quite a number of outbuildings. There were no man-sized openings near the ground.

"Here to cause trouble, Ragnar?" Otkel sneered. "You may have us outnumbered—but we have strong walls. And that's the bailiff next to you. Why don't you go back to the fair like a good little nithing, before you get in worse trouble than you already are."

"Why yes, Otkel—that's the bailiff. And the baronial guard for the north gate has its barracks only a few streets over. If we started a battle, they'd be on us like hornets."

"But I'm a peaceful man. To prove it, I've even made a poem in Thorolf's honor—and yours."

> Thorolf was a mighty leader;
> Foeman mine, but we could speak.
> Otkel hasn't Thorolf's courage—
> Shies from strong, and threatens weak.

Back in Surtsheim, Otkel's sister
Married well, to hearth and lands.
But the husband of that sister
Found his death from unknown hands.

Otkel cares not for the women.
Sister's husband lying dead,
Otkel slyly spread some silver,
Won his sister's own homestead.

Thorolf cared much for Matilda;
Wooing sometimes goes astray.
Thorolf, living, might yet win her.
Otkel threatened her, that day.

Thorolf worked when work was needed
Otkel often wasn't there.
But when silver was divided,
Otkel took an equal share.

Your band did some mighty trading
On the day of Thorolf 's doom.
Iron, dyestuffs, wine and glassware.
Then you had to haul it home.

Where was Otkel as this happened?
A Finn to me the story told.
On the Skraeling burial mound
Otkel raised an ill-made pole

Writ with strong runes poorly carven.
High Priest Gunnvald read the word.
"Bring me silver from the rich men.
I care not if they are cursed."

Thorolf was a rich man truly
Open-handed, spread his wealth.
Till the day his life had ended.
Where's his silver, where his pelf?

Otkel gave some to his Northmen,
Gained allegiance thus from them.
Gave more silver to the townsmen,
In the hope of buying friends.

Still and all, most of the silver
Ended up in Otkel's lap.
But not the brooch of Snorri Crow,
Which was hid within my camp.

Otkel worked in hidden fashion.
Thus to throw the guilt on me.
Raise the rune-pole, hide the cloak-pin
Don't get caught while doing these.

I say Otkel is a nithing
Dangerous in secret ways.
Scarcely harmful in the open
Once he's dead, he'll get no praise.

Otkel threatened, Thorolf calmed him,
Do men often change their ways?
Threats are certain, trouble surely
Follows Otkel all his days.

I have six years wanted Thorolf
Dead and buried, by my hand.
Now he's dead, and burnt on pyre,
Now we cannot have our stand.

I have lost an honest foeman,
Gained a craven one instead.
Otkel tried to use the bailiff
Sent him hunting for my head.

I'll take the man who tries to kill me
Brandish sword and shake the spear.
But the sneaking coward Otkel
Isn't someone whom I fear.

So I call you, nithing Otkel,
Once with courage in your life
Come and meet me on an island,
Let us settle up our strife.

Where the laws of Northmen govern,
Bringing nothing but a knife.
Fate will see who leaves the island,
Fate will see who leaves their life.

If I triumph, I'm rid of you.
Thorolf will be spared the shame.
If you triumph, then these Northmen
Have a leader worth the name.

As Ragnar spoke, Otkel had flushed first red, then white, then gone from the window. They could see the faces of his men following him with their gaze: to the side of the room, then back near the window. Ragnar finished his poem, and there was a long silence.

Ragnar saw motion inside the window. An arrow flew out, aimed at him. He caught it on his shield. The arrow was so fiercely driven that the arrowhead penetrated completely. Ragnar could see that it was one of his making. The men inside grabbed Otkel, took the bow away from him.

"You have good taste in arrowheads, Otkel. I congratulate you. Good taste, or a sense of humor—and here I thought you had neither." Ragnar walked carefully backwards, shield raised just in case. He reached the bailiff's side without incident.

Ragnar looked at Gervase, pointed at the shaft. "Maple."

They could see through the window that the men inside were agitated. Voices raised in argument, a dozen men shouting at once. Then somebody pulled the shutters closed with a crash. They heard a bar being slammed down inside to hold them shut.

Gervase looked at Ragnar in mild surprise. "Hm. Were all those things true? And did you just challenge Otkel to a fight to the death?"

"True, and only the half of it. A false weapon can bend or break when you use it. In a scorn poem, only truth will do. I think what happens to Otkel is now out of our hands. But if he comes through it all, I challenged him to holmgang. It's a way Northmen settle the strongest of grudges. 'Going to the island' is how it might be said in English. Two men go to an island, bearing weapons; only one returns."

The bailiff sighed. "I hope we don't have to take them by siege. Nobody would like that. It would inconvenience the merchants, annoy the baron, and somebody might get hurt."

"That probably won't happen. Otkel is too new as their leader, and he pushed things much too far. When he backed off from threatening Matilda, he lost his authority. I don't think Thorolf's men will stand by him now."

"He had that brooch hidden in your camp, you know."

"I suspected that, strongly enough to put it in the poem. It's the sort of thing he'd do, too clever by half. Thorolf would never have tried it. He was a straightforward enemy, was Thorolf."

"I'm surprised to hear you saying good things about Thorolf."

"Well, he was a strong, courageous leader. But he wanted to be leader of Surtsheim district, and Snorri Crow already had that position. So he and his men killed Snorri. I was one of Snorri's men, and naturally, we got together and tried to kill Thorolf and his faction. That was quite a battle. Eventually those of us who were left ended up at the Althing, where Thorolf and his men were declared outlaws...hold on, something is happening."

The gate of the warehouse creaked open, and twelve angry Northmen came out. They were wearing sheathed swords, and on their shoulders they carried chests and bags. Starkad wore his blanket as a cape. "If you need your blanket for a shroud, I'll send it back to you," he shouted hoarsely to somebody in the yard. The gate closed, and they heard it being barred.

They came up to Ragnar and the bailiff. Leif was in the lead, and spoke. "It now seems to all of us that Otkel was the sort to kill Thorolf for gain. In the days since Thorolf's death, certainly, he's done things—and had us do things—Thorolf would have scorned. He swore vengeance, by Odin, upon the man who shamed Thorolf. Right now, I think that's Otkel. He was a traitor to Thorolf's memory. Who knows how thoroughly he betrayed him in other ways? *Let* the vengeance fall upon him!

"But we gave Otkel our allegiance. It would have been against our word to seize him—and a violation of your law to kill him. We withdrew our allegiance, and left with our personal belongings. It's now our duty to help you take him. And I'll go to law on behalf of all us Northmen to gain our fair share of Thorolf's goods."

The three groups—the bailiff, Ragnar, Leif, and all the other men—surrounded the property. Nobody was going to leave.

"Open, in the name of the King!" Gervase bellowed. He pounded the knocker. "Open!"

They heard muttered voices on the other side of the gate. Otkel's voice raised in curses, and there was the sound of a smack, a cry of pain. A peasant voice rose: "We didn't hire on for this!" and other voices joined in. They could hear Otkel's curses diminishing in the distance, and the sound of the gate being unbarred.

The servants rushed out. One of them was bleeding from his nose. The troopers surrounded them. One gave a small handful of wool to the man with the nosebleed. The other servants clustered around. "There's nobody in there but Otkel," one said. "I'm not going back," another added, and "Thorolf was never like that!"

Leif, Dirk, and several of Thorolf's men got the servants well away from the gate and settled them down. Dirk started interviewing them. Servants always know more than their masters realize.

The bailiff, the troopers, Ragnar and his men, and most of Thorolf's men, drew their swords and went carefully through the gates. The yard was empty, and there were so many footprints that no particular set could be read. The bailiff and two troopers stayed by the gate to make sure nobody left that way, and he sent two more over to the side street to guard the windows.

Thorolf's men went into the warehouse with Ragnar and most of his men. Thorolf's men went up the stairs, and Ragnar's men spread out through the dimness of the lower floor.

Shadows loomed everywhere, and exotic smells. There were shelves of cloth, shelves of spices, stacks of wood, bales of wool. There must have been a hundred places to hide. Ragnar, Gunnar, and Ari stayed near the doors to keep watch on the yard and the outbuildings.

Horses stamped and whickered from the horse-barn. "He might try to escape on a horse!" one of the troopers shouted. Ragnar and several men went to surround the barn. But Gunnar didn't go with them. He thought he saw motion in one of the smaller outbuildings. He caught Ragnar's eye, pointed at the shed. "I see motion. I'll check if Otkel is in there."

He went over to the outbuilding. As he was coming up to the window, Otkel thrust his spear out and took Gunnar in the stomach. Gunnar hacked down with his sword at the same instant, and cut through the shaft of the spear and the wrist of Otkel's leading hand. The hand fell to the ground, and Gunnar pulled the spear out and dropped it to the ground also.

Gunnar walked back to the others, holding his belly and leaving a trail of blood. "Was Otkel there?" Ragnar asked him.

"That's for you to find out. For sure his spear was in there." Gunnar looked back at the ground by the window. "But if that is Otkel, you should be able to handle him, because I think he's a bit short-handed right now." With that, Gunnar fell to the ground and died. He looked almost as if he were sleeping.

"Right," Ragnar said, looking at Gunnar's body. "We've already lost one more man than we should have, and that's not Otkel's sword-hand on the ground. I don't see any reason to go in there and give him a chance to kill any more of us. And only a nithing would set the building on fire.

"I saw great-axes in the warehouse. Let's get them, and start cutting through the base of that building." Five men got axes, and did so. Other men took up their swords and came along, because they were expecting Otkel to burst through the door at any moment. He didn't.

While this was happening, Ragnar and several others were looking around. They found a longship mast stored on trestles above the ground, and carried it over to the outbuilding. They pushed it in the window, and then six of them pushed on the mast like sailors using a capstan to winch up the anchor.

Nothing happened. From inside they could hear a sword chopping. The mast was very thick, and nobody thought Otkel could cut it off in time. One of the men started singing a chantey. The others joined in. With every "Ho!" they surged against the mast.

The building creaked and swayed and twisted. The front wall, weakened at its base by the axes, broke outwards. The roof fell in with a crash and a cloud of dust. *Dust, even after the storm? It must have been a very good roof, to keep things dry enough for dust,* Ragnar thought. There was a muffled shout from inside, followed by a storm of coughs.

Men began hooking away the thatch of the roof with their great-axes. Soon Otkel was uncovered, quite alive and pinned by a roof-beam. He had dropped his sword and was clutching the stump of his left arm to stop the bleeding. He glared at them ferociously through dust-reddened eyes.

Ragnar stepped forward, and gestured in Gervase's direction. "I think the bailiff still has things to discuss with you. I thought you ought to know." He turned, and went back to Gunnar's corpse.

Chapter 15
Thursday: Another Pyre

Merchants had rented most of Matilda's horses earlier in the day. Matilda and Benedict had time for a happy argument about the similarities between horse traders and other merchants. That ended when Benedict noticed Ari and Atli riding across the bridge into the fairgrounds. "They're riding two of my horses from town. I'd better find out what's going on." He rose, and strolled toward Ragnar's booth. *They don't look cheerful,* he thought. *I hope there isn't trouble.*

The two men dismounted slowly at the entrance to Ragnar's booth. Olaf hurried over. Benedict arrived just as Atli was telling Olaf that "...Otkel killed Gunnar."

"**What?**" cried Olaf.

"What?" asked Benedict.

"When we got there, the bailiff was already at Thorolf's warehouse. Ragnar's scorn-poem turned the other men against Otkel. They and the servants left, and there was nobody in the yard except Otkel. When Gunnar found where he was hiding, Otkel thrust his spear out and killed him."

Olaf gritted between clenched teeth, "I'm going to get the rest of my men, and..."

"...and go there, and find the place locked and empty. The bailiff has Otkel and the warehouse, and our other men are preparing a funeral for Gunnar."

With a bleak smile, Ari said, "Besides, Gunnar can be proud in Valhalla. He had the finest last words I've ever heard of."

"Oh?"

"Ragnar told me to keep quiet on that until the funeral oration. Only he and I were close enough to hear."

Then the brothers turned to Benedict. "Ragnar wants you to take this whole thing to law for us. If Northlanding had paid more respect to the laws of Surtsheim, we wouldn't have had half this trouble, and Gunnar might still be alive. *Make* them pay respect."

"And now…" Ari and Atli turned toward the booth, "…it's time to gather grave-goods." They went in the door behind the empty display table, and Olaf followed. Benedict stood for a moment looking after them, then went to rejoin Matilda.

The sun was rising toward noon by the time Ari and Atli made it to the sacred grove. They were riding Benedict's horses still, leading a pack-horse with a brewing keg on its back, and other goods. They sacrificed blood to Odin's oak. Leif was standing there, trading glares back and forth with the priest.

At the top of the hill, Gunnar's body lay in state in the body of the wagon, set on a frame made for that purpose. His hands were folded over his sword, which still had Otkel's blood on it. Knute stood beside his friend, his face closed and one hand on the rim of the wagon frame. The brothers dismounted, and began to unpack the horse. Ragnar and the other men were stripped to their waists, carrying wood and building a pyre on the burnt-bare ground at the summit.

"What did you bring?" Ragnar asked.

"First, we got the spoon he used to fling boiling stew at the trooper."

Ragnar nodded.

"Then we talked with Olaf and his men, and decided that of all the things Gunnar did, we most loved the ale he brewed. We brought his brewing-keg, and we and Olaf gathered up all the drinking bowls and horns and cups. The keg still has the last ale of his brewing."

Ragnar pounded his fist into his palm. "Excellent! We can use that ale for the bragarfull oath!"

"And of course we have his bedroll, and the other things he carried around with him."

"Did you get a good cooking-knife?"

"We got Gunnar's knife."

"That's good, but it's not enough. If they have any sense at all in Valhalla, Gunnar will be as much a cook as a warrior." Ragnar turned to Knute. "Take one of these horses, go back to the booth, and get the finest cooking-knife in our whole inventory. We can put them both on the pyre."

Then Ragnar turned to the brothers. "I thought I saw Leif down there talking to the priest."

"It was more like arguing. Leif wants to come to the funeral, and the priest was refusing."

Ragnar shrugged. "Leif is a follower of the White Christ, and High Priest Gunnvald is a crusty old fellow. They don't get on that well. Gunnvald knows Leif was of Thorolf's faction. Maybe he doesn't want Leif to disturb us. But I've always thought Leif was the most decent of Thorolf's men."

Ragnar stroked his beard for a moment. The sun gleamed off his forehead, sweaty from working on the pyre. A droplet trembled on the tip of one of the forks of his beard, then fell. "Ari, go down there and tell the priest we want Leif at the funeral as a guest, and it won't cause any trouble. Then take two horses. You and Leif go to the abbey. Abbess Margaret and Father Hugh won't want to be at this ceremony. Their god is funny that way. But maybe John Freemantle would."

Ragnar thought a moment more. "Atli, borrow a horse from the Temple. Go into town and tell our friends Gunnar's pyre will be lit at sundown. And we should have a feast."

Atli agreed. "But where? If we have the feast in town, it'll be hard on our friends at the fairgrounds. If we have it at the fairgrounds, it'll inconvenience our friends from town. Either way, people will have to travel home long after sunset."

Ragnar nodded. "Perhaps we could have the feast here, *before* the funeral. It's not the custom, but this is *Gunnar's* funeral. *He* wouldn't mind if we put the food first, and everybody will have less traveling to do. Let's go see how High Priest Gunnvald feels."

The high priest agreed. The templefolk were used to funeral feasts—Northmen had them all the time. This one would be, at most, mildly unusual.

The Temple servants hauled out trestle tables for the food, and brought a roasting-spit for the fire circle. They even sold Ragnar one of their goats, and when Knute returned from the fair with the knife for Gunnar's pyre, he set right to work on the roasting. He used the knife he'd brought for the pyre—after all, the feast was in celebration of Gunnar. Atli was talking to Tony and Benedict, as well as spreading the news.

Benedict sent orders to the cooks at his warehouse: bake bread. Make treats. Bring butter. Get them to the Northmen's grove as rapidly as possible. They sent for Tony, who hitched up a horse to his wagon and brought his stores of ale, sausage, and cheese, plus all his bowls and mugs. By late afternoon, there was a substantial array of food set forth on the tables. The goat would keep roasting until it was needed.

People began to arrive. Benedict's servants had come with the bread, and were helping arrange the food. Tony was setting out bowls and mugs at the end of the tables near his wagon. Ragnar and the other men had finished stacking the pyre, and trailed down to get some food and drink after the work they'd done without a noon meal.

Dirk Cachepol arrived with—wonder of wonders—a clean-shaven face. He grasped Ragnar's shoulder. "I'm sorry it came to this. You and Gunnar and your men saved us a lot of grief. If you hadn't been there, this might be one of us."

"I'm not glad it was Gunnar, but there were omens. And once the Norns set their mind on a man's fate, it will happen that way. The High Gods themselves are at the mercy of Fate." Ragnar clasped Dirk's hand.

"The bailiff wanted to be here, but he's busy asking Otkel questions."

"That's useful. We'll be sending Gunnar off to Valhalla with our praises winging alongside. When Otkel dies, I want a complete list of his sins to travel with him." The two parted, as Ragnar saw Ari and Leif returning from the abbey with John Freemantle. They rode up, and dismounted. One of the Temple servants took their horses.

John Freemantle came up to Ragnar. "And just yesterday, Gunnar was alive and arguing with the gamekeeper. Is this what you were thinking about when you said their conversation sounded like trouble?"

Ragnar smiled bleakly. "I knew something bad was going to happen. I just didn't know what it would be, nor who it would happen to."

"No poem? Gunnar's death has you really out of sorts."

"I'm saving the poem for the funeral oration."

About then Matilda arrived, with riders on all her horses. Most of the riders were merchants from the fairgrounds, but there were servants and guards along also.

The feast began to take on a life of its own. Everybody crowded around the food and drink. Knute began carving off slices of goat, and putting them on platters for the table. Most people felt comforted by huddling into their own little groups.

Ragnar wandered from group to group, welcoming people, shaking hands, and listening carefully to the stories people told about Gunnar.

One group had memories from the fair of two years ago. "Do you remember that rain? Not as bad as the storm the other day, but it never let up." There were nods and murmurs of agreement.

"I'd just come down from Lakesend to do some trading. I was new to these fairs, but a lot of folk suffered right along with me. I hadn't saved enough dry wood, and water got under the edge of my tent to soak the wood I *had* put away. It was almost impossible to cook without dry wood. And I was getting tired of parched corn and jerky.

"Gunnar, bless him, had stored away plenty of wood. He put up a fly to keep the rain off his cook-circle, started a fire, and made an enormous cauldron of stew. He fed everybody that came to him. Just that one warm meal saved the whole fair for us. We had the strength to pull everything together, when the rain finally stopped."

"I remember that," one of the other fellows smiled. "Chicken stew it was, with a lot of vegetables. Not fancy, but he'd spiced and salted it just right."

"I always have a warm spot in my heart for a man that feeds me," a third added. "He didn't have to, we weren't at his steading."

Ragnar marked that down in his mind, and kept moving about.

"I was up by the Little Sea once, and stopped by that inn Gunnar and his parents keep. Never had such good food."

"Remember the time he killed that bear with his axe?"

"When we were carrying Gunnar home from the battle, after Otkel hit him from behind, he couldn't even stand up. But from his litter, he was scolding our cook over the seasonings."

"I knew him when he was young, and...."

* * *

As the day turned toward evening, Ragnar's men, and Olaf's, went up the burning-hill to the pyre. Carefully they lifted Gunnar's body, set him high on the prepared wood. They neatened his body and his hair, and adjusted the placement of his sword. Then they stood in a circle around the pyre, guards of honor for a well-liked member of their band.

The rest of the people, Gunnar's friends but not of his band, followed after.

Ragnar and Olaf went up the temple hill. With proper ceremony, each took a torch and lit it at the sacred fire. They paced slowly down the temple hill, and up the burning hill, bearing their torches. The sun, almost at the horizon, cast long shadows.

They approached the head of the pyre. Olaf handed his torch to Ragnar, and approached Gunnar's body. He took a small lantern from beneath his cloak, held it high. He turned to address the crowd.

"Gunnar never slept. All night long he stayed awake, watching over us, and this is the lantern he used. This lantern should go with Gunnar, rather than staying behind for some lesser use." Olaf lifted the lantern, set it by Gunnar's side, and returned to Ragnar. He took back his torch.

The man to Olaf's left stood forth, carrying his bowl. "Gunnar fed me, and gave me the best of ale. The memories I share with this bowl should not be diminished by food and drink from some other cook." He placed it by Gunnar's side.

The man to *his* left stood forth. He raised high a drinking horn. "In times of sorrow and times of joy, Gunnar's ale was a boon companion. From this day forth, no other drink shall touch this horn, save it be Odin's mead." He set the horn by Gunnar.

And so it went around the circle, each man praising Gunnar and putting his vessel by Gunnar's side. Finally the time to speak came around to Ragnar. He handed his torch to Olaf, went to the pyre by Gunnar's head. "Gunnar's sword is with him, covered with the blood of the man that slew him. He need take no other weapon with him to Valhalla. But in celebration of his life, here is his cooking-knife, and another fine knife as well." He put them by Gunnar, one at each side. Then he brought forth his drinking bowl, and put it there also. Finally he took a large Thor's Hammer of silver from around his neck, and placed it on Gunnar's chest. "Gunnar was a great companion. We'll not see his like again. Let this hammer guide him safely to the halls of Thor, the god whom he loved above all others."

Then Ragnar returned to his place beside Olaf.

The sun touched the earth. From the temple, the lur-horns sounded. Each of the men knelt down, and took up the torch lying at his feet. Ragnar and Olaf went around the circle sunwise, lighting each torch. Back at the head of the pyre, Ragnar and Olaf thrust their torches into the woodpile. "Now we send you to Thor," they said in a strong voice. The other men thrust forth their torches. "Now we send you to Thor."

The pyre, of oak and ash and elm, began to burn. Smoke and flames rose high, drifting to the west where the sun had disappeared. As daylight faded, shadows of the people in attendance were cast by the light of the fire. Everything was silent, save for the pops and crackling of the firewood. Their faces grew hot from the blaze, and everybody stepped back several paces.

Nothing lasts forever. The night grew darker as the fire burned low. Ragnar and Olaf turned to a tripod behind them, lifted a huge cup studded with garnets, and held it high. "The cup of Bragi, filled with the last ale brewed by Gunnar. Let us drink of the funeral ale, in memory of our friend and in praise of the god to whom he has gone." Ragnar lifted it to his mouth, drank deeply, then passed it to Olaf, who did the same.

Olaf began to carry the cup around the circle of men. Twice, he had to refill it from Gunnar's brew-keg. Finally it returned to Ragnar, who took it up and returned it to the tripod. He strode forth, faced the crowd.

"We have drunk the bragarfull ale. Now approaches the time to swear our oath."

"Gunnar was our friend and comrade. He traveled with us, took care of us, and because he never slept, he watched over us."

"Today, Otkel killed Gunnar. At the same time, Gunnar removed Otkel's hand, and gave him over to the bailiff. The fates of Gunnar and Otkel have been linked for six years, ever since the battle in which Otkel hit Gunnar from behind. Now they have been each others' doom."

"There have been omens, starting the night of the storm, when Gunnar saw the ravens of death circling over us. Before dawn today, Gunnar told me he saw a Valkyrie, who told him 'today would pay for all.'"

> Cattle die, kinsmen die.
> Someday we ourselves must die.
> I know one thing that never dies:
> The lasting fame of the storied dead.

"All men are mortal. Better to die young and healthy, in bold venture or battle, than to live into feeble age. And so Gunnar did. The rest of us were searching for Otkel in the warehouse and the stables, but Gunnar saw motion in another outbuilding. He went, alone, to check. Otkel thrust forth his spear and took Gunnar in the belly—but at the same time, Gunnar took Otkel's hand and spear with his sword. And then he returned to Ari and myself.

"Is Otkel in there?" we asked. And here Ari joined with Ragnar in chanting Gunnar's last words. As they ended with "... I think he's a bit short-handed right now" there was a murmur of praise from all the Northmen present.

"And so the time is here for the bragarfull oath. This is the oath I swear. None are truly dead, so long as their stories live. I will make and tell the saga of Gunnar the Unsleeping and Otkel the Short-handed. If you join in the oath, you can help by telling me your stories of Gunnar, and by telling those stories yourself."

Ragnar spread his arms wide, then made the sign of Thor's Hammer. He turned to the pyre. "We commend you to Thor, our friend, but we will keep your memory alive here in Midgard."

"And so we swear," all of Ragnar's and Olaf's men agreed in chorus.

"So be it," Ragnar and Olaf said. "And now our duty here is done." They turned to the bragarfull cup, and motioned to Gunnar's assorted friends. "Come, join us. Drink the ale, swear the oath, and keep Gunnar's memory." And most of the people

there did just that, though some who hadn't known Gunnar
well held back.

Then Ragnar and Olaf and their men began handing out
torches. People lit them from the embers of the pyre, and silently
went to the road leading back to their homes and beds. Behind
them, Temple servants gathered around the fire to tend it until
it burned its last.

Chapter 16
Friday: Saga

Birdsong. Sleepy voices in the distance, and daylight beginning to glow through the canvas of the roof. Ragnar came slowly toward wakefulness.

He rose, scrabbled his feet into sandals, wriggled into a work tunic, buckled on his belt with its sword, dagger, and pouch. Shuffling, not fully awake, he made his way to the door and out to the firepit.

Nothing was there. No breakfast, no Gunnar, nothing but a cauldron and a pit of ashes.

Ragnar made the sign of Thor's Hammer, then took buckets and headed to the river for water. He set a fire going beneath the cauldron. As the water was heating, he went inside the booth to rouse Knute.

Knute opened his bleary eyes. "What is it? Are we ready to start trading for the day?" Then he looked around, saw the other men still asleep and snoring. "That's not it, is it?"

Ragnar was sympathetic. "I'm afraid not. We have to eat, and we don't have Gunnar any more. You studied cooking with him, and are the best cook left among us. Even in times of sorrow, the business of life must go on. This, too, is a lesson a leader of men should take to heart."

Knute sat up, stretched, and made an unhappy face.

"I've started the fire, and set water to heating. We probably can't get breakfast ready before the trading starts. We'll have to finish off yesterday's bread. But could you have something ready for the noon meal?"

Knute shook his head and blew through his lips to make a sour noise. "Let me check our stores, to see what there is to work with."

"That's the place to start," Ragnar agreed. "I'll go over and see what I can get from Tony to help us break our fast."

Tony's wagon was still closed at his tavern. *I guess we tired him out and used up his stores at the funeral feast,* Ragnar thought. He listened carefully, and could hear faint snores coming from inside the wagon. *Best not to disturb him.*

Olaf was up by the time Ragnar got back to the booth. He was looking glumly at the cauldron as the water began to boil. "Water isn't much for breakfast." Then he brightened just a bit. "I traded for some tea, day before yesterday. It'll help." Olaf went back into his booth, came out with a smaller kettle and a brick of tea. He filled the small kettle from the cauldron, then began carving slivers of tea from the brick into the kettle. Its sharp smell rose.

About then, Knute came out carrying barley, lentils, and jerky. He poured the barley and lentils into the cauldron, then began cutting the jerky up into chunks and tossing them in also. "This ought to do for a while. Let's set some of the men to fishing. The king isn't nearly as possessive of his fish as he is of his deer." He gave the cauldron a good stir, then went back into the booth to get herbs and spices.

Ragnar had set up his display tables and organized them. He didn't get his usual help from Knute, who was busy cooking, but he had a surprising amount of energy for the job. *That tea is strong stuff,* he thought. *I'll have to get a supply of it myself.*

This was the last day of trading, and the twin threats of Thorolf and Otkel no longer hung over the fair. All the merchants were eager to get as much done as they could. Ragnar put aside his memories of Gunnar for the moment by trading hard. By noon, all of Ragnar's bulk iron was gone. The local cutlers, beltmakers, and scrimshaw workers had taken all the moose antler that was left after Captain Henry's purchase. The bailiff had sent messengers to purchase all the arrowheads. Ragnar thought that might be a kind of quiet apology for the suspicions. The knives and ax-heads were half gone. They'd gotten silver, copper, spices, wool, glassware, wine, and a chest full of small luxuries. They even had several ounces of gold. Olaf was doing well also.

About then, a band of Skraeling arrived, hoping to catch bargains at the end of the Fair. They brought beaver pelts with them, and buffalo robes. They were handsome and dignified, with their weatherbeaten faces and their fine deerskin clothes covered with decorations of brightly-dyed porcupine quills. One of them had feathers knotted in his hair. That was their sign of a leader. Olaf took one look at the pelts and immediately wanted them. There was always high demand for beaver pelts in Miklagard, and he was looking forward to selling buffalo robes there.

Olaf motioned them over. They spoke neither English nor Norse, but could talk eloquently enough with their hands. It soon was clear that they wanted hatchets and knives, and Olaf had none to trade. "Bring some knives and hatchets!" he called over to Ragnar.

Ragnar did, and the Skraelings' eyes lit up. They wanted a lot of plain knives, and a few very fancy ones, and the same with the hatchet heads. Ragnar, Olaf, and the Skraelings settled to bargaining, and worked out a three-way deal where the Skraelings got the knives and hatchets, Olaf got the pelts, and Olaf paid Ragnar in silver for his merchandise. They all clasped hands with a great show of smiles, and the Skraeling left as silently as they'd come.

That pretty well exhausted everything they'd brought to trade, so Ragnar and Olaf took down the display furniture and began to pack their new-won treasures for travel the next day.

In the afternoon, James Smith came by. He and Ragnar retired into the booth to talk in private.

"What's going to happen?" James asked. "You're free of suspicion now. But Gunnar's dead, and people in Surtsheim are going to want to know all the details. Should I prepare to get out of town in case the news gets back to Northlanding?"

Ragnar frowned. "You don't have much faith in my word. My judgement was that none of us would let people know you killed Thorolf. Here's what we can do: I won't tell anybody you killed Thorolf, and you won't tell anybody Otkel didn't."

"Can you keep to that, with everybody asking questions?"

"I'll just tell the simple truth. Thorolf is dead, and both the bailiff and Thorolf's men think that Otkel did it. Otkel tried to kill me, and I myself saw Otkel kill Gunnar. Otkel is in trouble for both killings, and will probably be hung."

James shivered. "Remind me never to get in a war of words with you."

"It was words that did Otkel in," Ragnar said. "That was a very dangerous poem I chanted."

They parted amicably, but somewhat coolly. It wasn't long before Dirk came by. "It's a sad day. I'll not forget the hospitality you and Gunnar gave me in the storm. And now he's dead. That might not have happened if we hadn't been suspicious of you."

"Dirk, sooner or later there was going to be a clash between Gunnar and Otkel. The two were fated for it. And if I hadn't *known* I didn't kill Thorolf, I would have suspected *myself.* Now Thorolf and Otkel will trouble people no more, and Gunnar has gone to the afterlife with fine last words. There are worse ways to die."

Dirk shook his head. "There are Northmen around here all the time. I should be used to it by now, but I think I'll never understand you."

"If you know Northmen at all, Dirk, you should know there are still matters to be taken care of. First, we should have Snorri Crow's brooch so we can return it to his family."

"We'll need it for Otkel's trial, but I don't see why you shouldn't have it after that."

"Give it to Benedict when you can. He'll take care of it until I can collect it. And then there's the matter of the wergild. Gunnar wasn't an important merchant, but he was an honest landholder with a good reputation and an illustrious lineage. His family should get a hundred ounces of silver as his man-price."

"That's a lot of silver. The baron may object, but Thorolf – and then Otkel – left behind enough merchandise to pay it a dozen times over. I'll argue the case for you."

"That's all I can ask of you," Ragnar said. The two men grasped hands.

"Come back this evening. We're having a small memorial for Gunnar."

"I will." And they took leave of one another.

Ragnar looked over and saw that Tony's tavern was open, and his wife Maude was there with the supply wagon, stocking it up for the afternoon's sales. He went there, and arranged for Tony and Maude to host a gathering that evening.

* * *

The tavern was full, and people spilled out around it: Northmen, and lots of merchants. Light spread from the central firepit, and was reflected back down from the trees and the canvas fly above. People had been drinking for some time. Even with his wagon replenished from the stores of his inn in Milltown, Tony was almost out of ale. Matilda was sprawled on the ground, leaning back against a tree – she'd been at the ice-wine again. Getting *out* of peril is at least as good a reason for a drunk as getting *into* peril, and safer as well. Benedict was leaning against the tree, smiling down at her; and Maude was watching them quietly from the wagon.

People were telling Gunnar stories, and Ragnar was listening carefully.

"... and then there was the time Gunnar ran into those Finns when he was travelling in the North...."

"Tell me about it!" said Knute. "I haven't heard that one!"

"Well, they offered to sell him a prime reindeer to help carry his supplies. Gunnar bargained them down, and got it for an excellent price as reindeer go. The Finns went off muttering and grumbling, but as soon as they got away from the camp they started laughing. They'd sold him a wild caribou, instead of a tamed reindeer. One of Gunnar's companions overheard them laughing."

"But Gunnar had the last laugh. Several days later the Finns came by again. The caribou was nowhere to be seen. 'How have you been getting along with your reindeer?' they asked."

"'He was delicious,' Gunnar replied. Then the Finns saw the hide stretched between two trees. They realized they'd sold Gunnar a food animal at a reasonable price, instead of playing a joke by selling him an unmanageable caribou. When they left, they were muttering and grumbling again. I have it on good authority that this time, they didn't start laughing once they were out of earshot."

The Northmen laughed, but few of them laughed as loud as the merchants in the crowd. Merchants like bargaining stories, and these merchants had taken on quite a bit of drink.

Tony stood high on one of the stumps. He spread his arms, called for attention. "Good people, you've drunk all there is to drink, and eaten all there is to eat. I'm closing for the night." He hopped down, shut the doors to the wagon, then he and Maude walked over to Ragnar. "It's been a long day."

"It has, indeed. And it would have been longer and harder without your help." Ragnar removed a small pouch from his belt. "I've already paid you the silver we bargained for, but here's more to thank you for being there in our time of need." He handed the pouch over to Tony, who smiled as he felt its weight, and tossed it to Maude for her to feel.

With the ale gone, the party was over. Merchants and porters began drifting away to their beds. Tomorrow would be busy with packing and departure.

Soon only Ragnar and Olaf's men were left, and a few of their friends. Benedict and Matilda were there, as were James Smith and Dirk Cachepol. They moved in closer to the fire where Ragnar stood.

Ragnar's voice took on the carrying note of a bard. "Yesterday, we took leave of our friend, Gunnar. Tomorrow, we take leave of Northlanding and this fair. But tonight is a night to tell the story of Gunnar the Unsleeping and Otkel the Short-handed." Everybody moved closer still.

"There was a man called Gunnar, who was the son of Ottar and Hilda. Ottar was a prosperous man who kept an inn on the northern shore of the Little Sea. He and his wife were famous cooks and hosts, and no cooks could take full pride in their food until Ottar and Hilda had approved of it. Ottar could trace his lineage back to Bjarni Herjolfsson, who discovered these lands we live in.

"It was the time of year that we gather together for the Althing, and Gunnar intended to be there to support Snorri Crow in an important matter. Gathering his travel gear, he set out on the road to the north...."

The End

www.ingramcontent.com/pod-product-compliance
Lightning Source LLC
Chambersburg PA
CBHW060748180626
46818CB00002B/503